Wordlife

THE CHESHIRE PRIZE FOR LITERATURE ANTHOLOGIES

Prize Flights: Stories from The Cheshire Prize for Literature 2003; **edited by Ashley Chantler**

Life Lines: Poems from The Cheshire Prize for Literature 2004; **edited by Ashley Chantler**

Word Weaving: Stories and Poems for Children from The Cheshire Prize for Literature 2005; **edited by Jaki Brien**

Edge Words: Stories from The Cheshire Prize for Literature 2006; **edited by Peter Blair**

Elements: Poems from The Cheshire Prize for Literature 2007; **edited by Peter Blair**

Wordscapes: Stories and Poems for Children from The Cheshire Prize for Literature 2008; **edited by Jaki Brien**

Zoo: Short Stories from The Cheshire Prize for Literature 2009; **edited by Emma Rees**

Still Life: Poetry from The Cheshire Prize for Literature 2010; **edited by Emma Rees**

Wordlife

Stories and Poems for Children from The Cheshire Prize for Literature 2011

Introduction by Toby Forward

Edited by Jaki Brien

University of Chester Press

First published 2012
by University of Chester Press
Parkgate Road
Chester CH1 4BJ

Printed and bound in the UK by the
LIS Print Unit
University of Chester
Cover designed by the LIS Graphics Team
University of Chester

Editorial Material
© University of Chester, 2012
Foreword, Stories and Poems
© the respective authors, 2012
Front cover image
© Russell Kirk

All Rights Reserved
No part of this publication may be reproduced, stored in a retrieval system or transmitted in any form or by any means without the prior permission of the copyright owner, other than as permitted by UK copyright legislation or under the terms and conditions of a recognised copyright licensing scheme

A catalogue record of this book is available
from the British Library

ISBN 978-1-905929-98-6

CONTENTS

Contributors	viii
Acknowledgements	xiv
Foreword by Toby Forward	xvi
A Wisp of Green Smoke *Catherine Jones* (winner)	1
Pirate through the Post *Ingrid Dean* (highly commended)	7
The Day that Grief Came to Stay *Barbara Holliday* (highly commended)	14
The Hoodie *Gabrielle Pearson Heavisides* (highly commended)	19
Maggoty Johnson *Angela Topping* (highly commended)	23
Pied Piper *Rachael Bate*	25
Counting Marbles *Sheila Blackburn*	29
Deadly Dancing *Hilary Bowen*	35

The Dog-father *Catherine Bruton*	42
The Wizards' Tea Shop *Pat Davies*	46
Going for Gold *Derek Matthews*	50
Colour Coding *Jo Mayers*	51
Exam Room *Don Nixon*	54
Frozen *Paul Palmer*	55
Scarce *Tanya D. Ravenswater*	58
Mermaid's Purse *Patricia Roberts*	63
Fake Blood and Bullies *Rosamund Roberts*	67
The Extraordinary Inventions of Victor Vanash *Lisa Jane Rowlands*	73
Arthur and the Mountain *Nicola Russell-Johnson*	77

Hester's Hands   84
Beverley Sims

Forevermore   89
Andrew Smith

The Evacuee   94
Naomi Walker

Lion   97
Stephen Wrigley

CONTRIBUTORS

Rachael Bate works at the University of Chester. In her spare time she enjoys baking cupcakes, walking, especially with her dog, Tamar, and is currently working on a manuscript that may possibly and hopefully one day become a children's novel. Her influences are Alan Garner, John Masefield and C.S. Lewis.

Richard Bennett (judge) is a former primary teacher and headteacher with over forty years' experience of the primary sector. He has worked as a teacher educator in various roles, most recently as a senior lecturer in education at the University of Chester. He has written several books, chapters and articles on aspects of ICT and technology in education.

Sheila Blackburn is a semi-retired primary teacher, now working part-time teaching French, Art and tutoring pupils for Literacy. Reading and writing are still her favourite pastimes; she also loves gardening and floristry. She is involved in projects in Queens Park in Crewe and particularly in educational developments and opportunities.

Hilary Bowen resides in Macclesfield, Cheshire. At age 21, she discovered that a music degree just about qualified her to flip burgers at McDonalds. Instead, she decided to teach piano and has been doing so for the last twenty years. Her passions are reading and writing. She lives in her imagination and emerges occasionally to walk the dogs.

Jaki Brien (editor) regards judging the Cheshire Prize and editing the anthology as two of the most enjoyable parts of her job at the University of Chester. Recently she was

Contributors

seduced to the dark side and wrote an academic text book for undergraduates but has now returned to the light and is concentrating on children's fiction.

Catherine Bruton was brought up in Lymm, but now lives near Bath with family. Her novel *We Can be Heroes* was nominated for the Carnegie Medal, longlisted for The Branford Boase Award and The Redbridge Children's Book Award and shortlisted for The Centurion Book Award. Her second *Pop!* (June 2012) is inspired by her North West upbringing.

Pat Davies was born on the Wirral and now resides in Liverpool. She has worked in a variety of sectors and has recently completed a degree as a mature student. She has two short stories for adults currently in print. Pat is now finishing her first novel and developing several stories for children.

Ingrid Dean grew up in Pembrokeshire then attended university and qualified as an English teacher. When she moved to Cheshire she became an Education Facilitator in a Tudor Hall. She has written and directed numerous plays for a Children's Drama Group and at present is engaged in writing a novel.

Toby Forward (judge) lives in Crosby with his wife, Jean. They have two daughters. He has been writing since 1987, when he began with stories broadcast by BBC Radio 4. Since then he has published books for all ages, from picture books to adult fiction. At present he is working on a quartet of junior fiction novels for Walker Books, the 'Flaxfield' series. *Dragonborn* was published in January 2011, and *Fireborn* in

Wordlife

July 2011. *Doubleborn* and *Starborn* will complete the series in 2012.

Barbara Holliday grew up in Ellesmere Port and still has a copy of her first illustrated story, 'Super Cat', written at the age of six. She gained an English Literature and Creative Writing degree from Manchester Metropolitan University in 1993. She now works as a Research Administrator in the Faculty of Health and Social Care at the University of Chester, is a wife and mother, and in her spare time likes to write, research her family history and bake cakes.

Russell Kirk gained his Integrated Arts degree at Dartington Hall. His interest in performance and processional arts led to his current post of Artistic Director of the Chester Midsummer and Winter Watch. He has recently turned to writing and illustrating; *St George and the Dragon* was published in March 2012 and *The Star Makers* is due out next spring.

Catherine Jones (winner) was born and raised on Tyneside, spent part of her childhood overseas but has lived in Cheshire longer than anywhere else. She is currently a local authority Conservation Officer. Inspired by her love of the past, Catherine started writing short stories last summer when her husband and daughters weren't looking. She hopes her success in the Cheshire Prize bodes well for a literary future.

Derek Matthews, who lives in Alsager, South Cheshire, is a member of 'Keele Poets at Silverdale'. His passion for writing poetry flowered in early retirement, following his

Contributors

career as a shipping agent. Grandchildren inspire his writing of children's poetry.

Jo Mayers is a graduate of the University of Warwick, where she studied English Literature and took a course in Creative Writing. Since then she's moved back to her home town of Macclesfield, and completed courses in counselling skills. She writes from home, in her spare time.

Don Nixon began writing poetry and short stories a few years ago and, since having a story published in the Cheshire prize anthology in 2005 has gone on to successes in various competitions in Britain and Italy. Two of his crime stories will be published by Bridge House Press later this year.

Paul Palmer is a 46-year-old freelance cartoonist living in Ellesmere Port with his wife and two teenage sons with whom he shares an interest in music and football. New to writing without pictures he has found himself drawn to tackling issues of loss and bereavement.

Gabrielle Pearson Heavisides appears to have settled in Chester. She has reached a stage in life where there are no pressing demands being made on her which she is finding rather odd. She is, however, using the freedom of this to find new ways to amuse herself, focusing particularly on mindfulness and creative writing.

Tanya D. Ravenswater is a writer of fiction and poetry for children and adults. She enjoys working in schools to encourage children with their creative writing. Born in Northern Ireland, Tanya has lived in Cheshire for almost twenty years. She is inspired by nature, childhood, family and exploring the extraordinary within "ordinary" life.

Patricia Roberts has taught English in Cheshire for a long time and loves sharing stories with children. She loves being by the sea and is fascinated by poems and stories of shipwrecks, islands and mermaids. She lives in an old farmhouse with her family and a much loved stripy cat.

Rosamund Roberts lives in Cheshire with her husband and three sons. Before computers took over the world, she was privileged to teach young minds. Now she runs a laundrette, café and taxi service. She also spends time peeling her 10-year-old son off the computer so that she can write.

Lisa Jane Rowlands is a teaching assistant from Chester who credits her students with being the inspiration for her work. Until now, her humorous verse and often accompanying illustrations have served only to entertain friends and family. However, she remains hopeful that they will be afforded a wider audience in future.

Nicola Russell-Johnson was born in Chester but worked in Europe, Asia and South America for five years teaching English. She's now settled back in the UK with her husband and Doog the infamous call duck and works as a freelance writer. She's also a postgraduate student, is interested in Second World War aviation and enjoys playing the ukulele in her free time.

Beverley Sims was born in Stockport in 1967, and has been a poodle groomer, graphic designer and curriculum leader. She now works as a copywriter and EFL teacher just south of

Contributors

Rome, where she battles with summer mosquitoes and winter snows. Her faithful companion is her dog, Reuben, who is not a poodle.

Andrew Smith lives and works in Chester with his wife and daughter. He first started writing while living in Japan, at first because he couldn't understand the television, and then because he enjoyed it. He primarily writes in the science fiction and crime genres, but also does some freelance magazine writing.

Angela Topping writes for both children and adults. Of her eight published poetry collections, two are specifically for children, *The New Generation* (Salt, 2010) and *Kids' Stuff* (Erbacce, 2011). Her next collection, *Paper Patterns*, is forthcoming from Lapwing Press. A former teacher and lifelong Cheshire resident, she now works as a freelance author and writer in schools.

Naomi Walker has a legal background, but since having her two children has decided on a career change. She is in the second year of her English Literature degree and is loving every minute of it. She enjoys writing and is working on a children's book.

Stephen Wrigley has recently moved south from Wirral, pursuing children and a grandson. He writes poetry across a range of subjects and his latest collection, *A Ring of Stones*, published by Appin Press, Birkenhead, reflects on worship. Illustrated with line drawings, it features churches and sites on the Continent and in the UK, particularly in the Romney Marsh area, near where he now lives.

ACKNOWLEDGEMENTS

It always seems a little unfair to me that the editor gets an undue share of the accolades when so many people work together on The High Sheriff's Prize for Literature. In an attempt to redress this imbalance my thanks go to:

Our splendid sponsors, Bank of America, whose support means so much to us all. I would also like to thank Sarah Griffiths, managing editor of the University of Chester Press, for her remarkable patience and energy, and Lynda Baguley, from the Corporate Communications team, for her ability to juggle metaphorical flaming torches whilst appearing completely composed. The members of staff of the University's LIS Print Unit and Graphics team are always the invisible heroes of the year: my thanks go to them.

I'd also like to thank Russell Kirk for kindly allowing us to reproduce one of his wonderful pictures on the cover of this anthology.

The judging team enjoys reading the entries so much that perhaps they don't need thanks. I am very grateful to them for their enthusiasm and their depth of insight into what children enjoy. Emma Dollard, Brendan Hoare, Helen Holt and Claire Warner judged the preliminary stages of the competition, finding our finalists, all of which appear in this book. At the final stages of judging, children's author Toby Forward and my colleague, Rik Bennett, shared the delights and anguish of sifting through the excellent entries to find the winner: I am very grateful to them both.

I also have to thank Rik for the anthology title, *Wordlife*. Finally, and most importantly, I would like to thank all the writers who breathed life into the words you'll find in this book. 'A Wisp of Green Smoke' is a very worthy winner of The High Sheriff's Prize for Literature this year but all the

Acknowledgements

other stories and poems are brimming over with the life and liveliness that brings children to a love of reading. I am sure all readers will join me in thanking our authors.

FOREWORD

I haven't always been a huge fan of prizes and competitions, especially for writing. The Man Booker judges seem to get it wrong almost as often as they get it right. There are questions about whether the judges are competent, questions about how you rate a thriller against a work of historical fiction, how you judge a traditional work against one which explores the technique of writing: too many variables to allow a clear and uncontested decision. And that's before you even say that so-and-so has been on the shortlist three times and so she ought to win this year. Often it seems to me that the only prizes and competitions should be for greyhound races and bare-knuckle street fighters.

Well, I used to think like that. I've mellowed a little over the years. At the very least, writing competitions do some things which I think are unarguably good. They encourage people to have a go. People who've often thought they'd like to put something on paper, but are daunted by the difficulty of getting published, know that if they enter a competition someone will read what they've produced. Not just read it, but read it sympathetically, eagerly. It's true of me, and I think of all the judges here, that I wanted to find some really good writing.

Competitions increase interest in writing. They raise its profile. They move the eyes from the television screen and the games console to the page. And I think that's a good thing. They engage debate. They make people ask what it is that makes one story good and another not so good. Even when they get the answer wrong, and they sometimes do, it's worth considering the question.

Writing is a lonely and sometimes dispiriting business and the opportunity to be involved in a prize like this can lift

Foreword

the heart, especially if, at the end of it, there's a cash prize, or a place in a published anthology. So, I'm honoured and delighted to be involved in judging The High Sheriff's Prize this year. And I'm especially grateful to have worked alongside Jaki Brien and Rik Bennett.

We enjoyed many of the stories and poems. Well done to all who entered, whether they won or were included in the anthology or not. I'm pretty sure that, at least as far as the outright winner is concerned, we got it right. 'A Wisp of Green Smoke' by Catherine Jones is an elegant, assured and convincing story. I want to read more by this writer, and I'm sure I shall.

Toby Forward, November 2011

Editorial note: I'm delighted that Toby Forward's latest book *Dragonborn* has recently been nominated for the CILIP Carnegie Medal for children's literature.

A WISP OF GREEN SMOKE

Catherine Jones

I lowered myself from the sill, the floorboards protesting under my feet, and paused, sniffing the air. The stink of harbour fish and the dirty odour of salt and seaweed followed me in, filtering through the casement to meet a silence laced with the vapours of paraffin, linseed oil and animal glue. Its notes drifted towards me now, above these powerful fumes, just like the first breath of green smoke gulped into my wailing lungs. We were all born with its scent in our nostrils, but I cannot think it eased my mother's birthing pangs as the women told her it would. Those tarry traces of smouldering jet wrenched at my insides, a visceral tug of memory that left me breathless.

"Davey! Move!" Sophia's hiss set my heart pounding in my ears.

"Sorry!" I whispered, grabbing her skinny elbow as she slid through the window.

"See. Told you it would be easy." I saw a flash of her white teeth.

"Hardly!" I snorted. "It would have been easier to use the door. Nobody locks up round here."

"Half of Whitby would have seen us if we came through the yard. You're in enough trouble already."

"I know. But I don't fancy going back across that roof." I shivered, remembering the groan of the timbers and the loose pantiles scraping against each other as we scaled the ridge, the ground sickeningly far beneath the eaves.

"Don't you want your boots?" she demanded.

"Of course I do!" My buttocks still smarted from the beating my mother had given me when I came home barefoot. "But how can you be sure they're here?"

Her puff of exasperation misted against my skin. "'Cos I followed him from the beach."

There was a scratch and a fizz as a match flared in her cupped hand. I screwed up my good eye until it became accustomed to the flame. The other was swollen shut anyway, the tender flesh tight with purple blood from the impact of Abel Mortimer's fist.

Sophia withdrew a candle stub from her apron and lit the wick.

"Are you mad?" I asked, hoarse with incredulity. "Someone's sure to see us!"

"Best be quick then."

She cast the spent match into the shadows and slipped the matchcase back into her pocket. One fine brow arched and the hint of a challenge lifted the corner of her mouth. I felt a sudden lurch in my chest, my breath catching as the flickering light played over her delicate features. I would have kissed her. If I'd had the courage.

I scanned the benches fitted with their lethal array of grindstones and milling discs, every worktop scattered with chisels, saws and blades. It didn't take Sophia long to find my boots, stowed behind a treadle that drove one of the wheels.

"Let's go," I urged.

"Not until I find my jet."

I could understand why she wouldn't leave without it. Even the shore had been reluctant to give it up until I loosened its greedy suck with my finger. Although I'd seen its crisp black edge first I'd let her believe it was her discovery, laughing at her delight when she wiped away the

A Wisp of Green Smoke

smears of wet sand and saw its surface, dappled with the imprint of ancient leaves. It was the kind of piece any jet-worker would covet; the kind I'd often told her I would save until my apprenticeship was served, when I'd have the skill to work it into something truly extraordinary.

But Abel had other ideas. Sophia's face had been in the sand before she felt the shove that knocked her off her feet. The jet had tumbled from her hands and she sat, winded, wiping strings of gritty saliva from her chin. I launched myself at him, but one casual blow was enough to floor me, too. Scooping up the jet with a vicious laugh, he sauntered away.

"I hope you burn in Hell for that!" I'd yelled. It was only as we reached the path to the town that I realised the rotten thief had taken my boots as well.

"This isn't even proper jet!" My lip curled in disdain as I sifted through the samples on Abel's bench – the French glass the artisans scorned, and the cheap Spanish stuff, soft and dull. Its blurry facets wouldn't keep their shine like Whitby jet, not for all the rouge in town. The clatter of tin turned us both to statues. Beads of sweat sprang out on my forehead and Sophia gasped in horror at the blood-red burst that had soaked my shirt as my sleeve dragged the little jug of polish to the floor.

"I didn't see it!" I cried in dismay, my hand flying to my bruised eye.

We both heard the creak of hinges from the yard below. "Out!" she mouthed urgently.

I hauled myself through the window, reaching to pull her up behind me. My eyes widened in panic as she snuffed out the candle in a sizzle of moistened fingertips and waved me away. The last thing I saw before I ducked out of sight was her glare of warning as she disappeared beneath a bench. I heard the latch snap open and willed my feet not to slip as I scrambled desperately out over the rooftop.

My shirt left a trail of seawater over the cobbles behind me. I prayed the drops weren't red. Sophia was leaning against the wall of my yard, my boots slung around her neck like a ridiculous, oversized piece of jewellery. Relief flooded over me that she was safe – and that I wouldn't have to clamber back over Josiah Mortimer's roof to rescue her.

"If you'd wanted a necklace I'd have made you one!" I joked.

"Except jet's for grieving, ninny!" She looped the boots over her head and held them out to me. I wound the laces around my hand, a lopsided grin spreading across my face.

"Maybe you'll need some mourning beads after all. Abel's going to kill me tomorrow."

"That's not all he'll be sore about."

My brow furrowed as I peered into her shadowy face. Suddenly, I felt her cool fingers against my knuckles as she placed an object in the centre of my palm. It was light and warm, and I swear I even felt it crackle when it touched my skin, discharging the buzz of static it had collected from the worn cotton inside her pocket. Sophia must have sensed its power, too – that spark of danger that was both its attraction and, sometimes, the germ of its own destruction.

I gasped. "You found your jet!"

"Not mine. Yours. Save it for something special."

I opened my mouth to protest but she folded my fingers around the jet's smooth contours. My heart swelled before a shiver of apprehension raised the hairs on my bare arms.

"What about Abel?"

"Forget Abel," she murmured. "He won't say anything."

I was about to ask her how she could be so sure when her kiss took the words right from my mouth. I stared at her

A Wisp of Green Smoke

in surprise, unable to explain the unwanted feeling of confusion welling inside me. And then she was gone, melting silently into the maze of streets, as insubstantial as a mist from the sea.

"My George reckons the jet sparked it off, just like that."

"Wouldn't be the first time." The fishwives nodded in agreement, craning their necks to see past the onlookers who had gathered to gawp at the smoking hulk of Josiah Mortimer's workshop. "Though he swears he didn't keep much on the premises."

"That figures!" She lifted an ironic eyebrow. "They say he's never worked a real piece of Whitby jet since Prince Albert died!"

They stifled their amusement when they recognised Abel's tear-streaked face scowling at them.

One cleared her throat. "Anything we can do, son ..."

Abel pushed past them. Our eyes connected and my heart hammered with fear that he would twist my collar round his fists and slam me against the wall. Instead, he shot me a furtive glance.

"Don't tell Da I took it. Please," he mumbled.

"I won't ... " I replied, puzzled. He merely nodded and slunk away like a kicked dog. Then it struck me: he blamed himself! He really thought the stolen jet had burned his father's workshop down! He hadn't even noticed I was wearing my boots ...

I threaded my way through the crowd, finding Sophia near the front. We stood together, surveying the blackened ruins. Every now and then, tiny curls of sulphurous green smoke rose from the wreckage. I turned to Sophia with an uneasy smile, the bridge of my nose wrinkling into an unspoken question which she only answered with the enigmatic curve of her own mouth. This time I couldn't pretend the wisps of burning jet were an instinctive recollection of my birth, or even of the moment I cracked the casement and dropped into Josiah Mortimer's workshop. What made my stomach writhe was the memory of those same little breaths of jet-smoke weaving through Sophia's hair – the scent I remembered inhaling the instant she touched her lips to mine.

PIRATE THROUGH THE POST

Ingrid Dean

Mrs James sighed, "Trouble is," she muttered, "I just haven't got to grips with the workings of that internet."

"Talking to yourself now, young Deborah. Not a good sign."

Mrs James turned to face her Uncle Oswald who had clambered in through the kitchen window. "The trouble is I'm trying to order a parrot from the 'Pick a Parrot.com' website but am having no luck at all."

"Have you asked Rob?"

"Not yet."

"Afraid you'll lose face, eh?"

She blushed. "So what if I am; it comes to something when a mother's got to ask her son's help in ordering something as simple as a model parrot from an internet website."

"I tell you what; I'll show you now and he need never know."

Putting her doubts and memories of past disasters to the back of her mind she murmured, "How kind."

"What does he want with a parrot anyway, noisy birds the lot of them?"

"Not a real parrot Uncle, a model one to wear with his pirate costume."

"Ah you need that "Parrot through the Post.com' website."

"That's the one."

"Should be easy; let's start."

Half an hour later Mrs James had been instructed in the art of shopping through the internet. Once Uncle Oswald left with a cheery goodbye she sat back with her laptop and ordered the parrot.

"Hey Mum, what's up?"

She hurriedly closed the website and pushed her laptop underneath a cushion. "Hello Rob, nothing's up. I've just been ordering a parrot for your father's pirate costume."

"Cool, Mum. Hope you pressed the right keys on the computer; we don't want Dad ending up with a ballerina's tutu or a tiara or something do we?"

"I'm not an idiot, you cheeky monkey, and I wasn't born yesterday."

Rob just looked at his mother and grinned widely. "How soon before it comes?"

"They guarantee twenty-four hours' delivery."

"Do I need to take time off school?"

The earnest expression on his cherubic face was not convincing enough to fool his mother. "Ha! Ha! Forget it Rob. I'll wait in tomorrow so you can go to school."

"Oh well, it was worth a try."

"Never mind that nonsense, you can help me find a hiding place for the parrot when it arrives."

The words, 'if it arrives,' echoed silently between them but were never uttered.

The following morning the front doorbell rang, interrupting the family's breakfast. Rob and his mother raced to be first to meet the postman. He unloaded a huge, squirming parcel from his van.

"Mum how big a parrot did you order and was it meant to be a live one?"

"Of course not, can you imagine your dad coping with a live parrot on his shoulder?"

Pirate Through the Post

"It looks alive to me Mum. I think it's fighting to get out of the wrapping. Have you noticed what a struggle the postman is having with it?"

Mrs James peered over her son's shoulder saying in a puzzled tone of voice,

"Err; maybe he's not very strong."

Meanwhile the sweating postman managed to haul the quivering parcel to the front door.

"Mrs James?"

"Yes."

"I've never experienced such a difficult delivery before. Sign here please."

She took the pen from the postman and signed her name while smiling apologetically at him.

"Sorry to hear that."

Sighing he heaved the quivering parcel over and trundled back to his van mopping his brow as he did so.

"Zounds!"

Rob and his mother exchanged puzzled glances. "You never told me you'd ordered a talking parrot."

"That's because I didn't."

"But, but I heard a voice say, *'zounds'*."

They turned quickly to open the parcel. The tape was difficult to cut but eventually they succeeded and a figure jumped out. It wasn't a parrot. It was a full-blown pirate looking somewhat dishevelled. He was tall, black-haired and fierce looking.

"Who are you?"

"I am the pirate you ordered, wench. Name is Geoffrey."

"But, but I didn't order a pirate; I ordered a parrot." Mrs James's voice expressed her bewilderment.

"Oh Mum, you must have punched in 'Pick a Pirate.com'."

"I was following your Great-Uncle Oswald's instructions but obviously I took a wrong turn."

"Who be you calling a wrong turn?"

"Mum wasn't calling you a wrong turn."

"She said she'd taken a wrong turn."

"But she didn't mean you. She only meant she'd given the wrong order."

Mrs James nodded, "That's right. I meant to order a parrot."

"Can you really order parrots on the internet? I've tried that there home-shopping channel but they only provides them there pesky model ones. No self-respecting, fearsome pirate would go down that road." He shivered.

Another thought occurred to Rob causing him to turn to face Geoffrey who was tugging on his black beard.

"How long will you be staying with us?"

"My contract specifies ten days. Be that long enough for you?"

"Certainly is."

"What do that mean, Boy?"

Faced with a terrible scowl descending on the pirate's face Mrs James hastened to add, "Only that it's good you're here for ten days because it means you can join us on our family outings."

The pirate smiled happily. *"I ain't never been invited on a family trip before. Where be we going and will I need my astrolabe and my octant?"*

Rob gazed at his mother in horror. "Where are we going Mum? And will Dad be pleased about our unexpected guest?"

His mother looked hard at him. "Of course he will."

"Well how about a visit to Cornwall then. We could take a boat trip; I reckon Geoffrey would enjoy that."

Mrs James nodded in agreement. "I think that's an excellent idea Rob. Would you enjoy a trip to the seaside Geoffrey?"

"Happen I would Mrs, and if that be our destination I will need my astrolabe so we can navigate by the sun and that there Pole Star. That way I be able to find all me friends and others."

"I'm pleased to hear it."

Really, thought Mrs James, for a pirate his behaviour isn't so bad. It was more comical than threatening. If only we can calm him down before Brian comes home everything should be fine. Rob looked from the grinning pirate to his mother and wondered.

"I reckon young Rob that with all this travelling back to Cornwall I can revisit all the places Blackbeard and I fought over and show all me mates it's me what's most fearsome."

Rob did not like the sound of this and just hoped Geoffrey would calm down before his dad came home.

It wasn't long before Brian James returned and met a calm Geoffrey. Brian liked him because he had always

Wordlife

longed to be a pirate and believed Geoffrey might advise him on how to dress and act as a pirate should. He approved of inviting him to accompany them to Cornwall.

The following day the family found themselves on the London to Penzance train. The weather was beautiful which cheered them all up. It's hard to be miserable when the sun shines and the sky is blue. Rob was pleased to see his parents so relaxed but at the back of his mind lay a niggling doubt. Geoffrey was always so jolly. It didn't seem right. He felt that a pirate who was determined to become more fearsome than Blackbeard had no right to be so friendly and jovial. He looked across at the three of them. It seemed pointless to mention his worries. He decided to wait and observe Geoffrey's behaviour.

On Thursday morning Rob had an uncomfortable sensation at the bottom of his stomach. He crawled down to breakfast to be met with the news that they were all booked on the Scillonian to visit the Isles of Scilly. The thought of travelling on a flat-bottomed boat was almost enough to bring on a state of relapse. His mother offered to wait with him while the others enjoyed the trip.

"No Mum, honestly I'll be fine."

"Ahh, that's a good lad. Reckon we'll all enjoy some sea air."

"He's up to something," muttered Rob to himself, "but what?"

It didn't take long for the truth to be revealed. They had only just left Penzance Harbour when Geoffrey mentioned persuading the captain to change course.

"When did you meet him?"

Brian's face expressed everybody's surprise.

Pirate Through the Post

"I'm a'goin' to meet him today so as I can commandeer this here ship. I needs him to change course to the Caribbean."

"He may not have time to talk."

"Happen he'll make time. He'll have no choice once I take command."

They watched with dismay as Geoffrey sauntered towards the Bridge.

"This has got to stop!"

Rob stared at his mother who was taking her mobile out of her bag. He wondered what she was about to do. He soon found out. Alerted by a loud whirring noise he looked up to see a huge helicopter with a postman descending from it.

"I've come for Geoffrey."

"I be here. Do your worst."

Rob watched Geoffrey being hauled up into the helicopter. He was brandishing his cutlass and shouting something down to Rob. Laughing, he rejoined his parents.

"Your mother contacted 'Return a pirate.com'."

"It worked Dad. They've collected him. He says he doesn't blame you and he's left a present behind."

They ran to Geoffrey's cabin and there on his bed was a model parrot with a note pinned on its chest. The words read *"Please take care of this here parrot."*

THE DAY THAT GRIEF CAME TO STAY

Barbara Holliday

It was the day of his Dad's funeral and George was staring angrily at the sympathy cards on the sideboard. The net curtain was blowing in the breeze from the open window and George was busy wishing that everyone would just go home when all of a sudden, something bowled in through the open window and hit George in the stomach with such force that he slid across the floor and crashed into his Dad's empty armchair. Whatever had hit him was warm, breathing and clinging tightly around his middle.

George looked down. Curled up next to his stomach, about the size of a football, was some sort of creature. He couldn't see it very clearly but George wasn't comfortable having something strange and alive attached to him, so he tried to remove it. But no matter what he did, it just wouldn't budge.

George's Mum came into the room to see what all the commotion was about and when she saw George she gave him a reassuring hug and stroked the creature on the head.

"It's OK," she said. "It's Grief."

George looked at her aghast. Didn't she think that this was weird? He certainly did.

"You'll get used to him," said Mum. "He came to see me when Granddad died."

George shivered.

Losing Dad had made George do and think some strange things. For example, a week after his Dad had died, George was on the bus coming back from town when he swore that his Dad was waiting at the bus stop outside the hospital. He had leapt off the bus but when George had

The Day that Grief Came to Stay

gotten close to the man, he was actually nothing like his Dad at all.

Now George was lying in bed thinking that he must have imagined Grief coming to visit when he tried to roll over. Suddenly a noise, crossed between a cat growling and a deflating bagpipe, came from George's middle and he realised that he had squashed Grief.

"Sorry!" said George.

Grief looked up from George's middle and suddenly spoke in a thin, nasal voice, "Your Dad's not dead." George looked at the strange creature in shock, his heart racing.

"He's in Ward 42," it said.

George's heart and stomach flipped liked a kipper and he knew exactly what he had to do.

After school, instead of going straight home, George and Grief got off the bus at the hospital and walked up and down corridors until they found Ward 42. Luckily it was visiting time. George carried Grief with him as he checked every bay but there was no sign of his Dad. George read all the names on a big white board by the nurses' station and even asked a nurse, but sadly Grief was mistaken.

The very next day Grief spoke again. "It's your fault he's dead," he said.

George gasped because Grief was absolutely right. George's stomach flipped. He felt sick and very guilty.

"You wished him dead," Grief tormented.

George started to panic and his breathing was getting too fast. His Mum gently took George to one side and helped him to calm his breathing down.

"What's the matter, my darling?" said his Mum wrapping her arms around him with Grief in the middle.

"I killed Dad!" George blurted out and began to shake and cry. "I wished him dead when I was cross with him!" said George sobbing.

George's Mum held him and Grief tightly and gave them a big loving hug.

"Shhhh. There now. Dad was poorly my darling. You're definitely not to blame." She kissed his and Grief's heads and held and rocked them until they fell soundly asleep. "You did nothing wrong my darling," she whispered into his dreams.

But his dreams didn't believe her and George woke up in the middle of the night, rocking back and forth and crying "I want him back". He wailed and sobbed and pleaded with Grief. "I'll swap all of my toys and my entire computer game collection if you can just bring him back."

Grief shook his head. "Can't," he whispered.

George looked into Grief's big sad eyes and their faces both crumpled and they cried together. Not just normal tears, but big, uncontrollable salty tears.

They cried all through the night. They cried when they were awake. They cried when they were asleep and when they woke up in the morning there was a deep sea of salty tears in the room and the water swelled and grew and washed them clear out of the window on a wave that sent them crashing down off the edge of a vast waterfall, down and down until they rushed into the river below. Suddenly they began to spin inside a swirling whirlpool and were carried, further and further down until they fell into a deep, dark pit and came to a complete stop.

George lay still, unable to move. Grief crawled up George's chest and gripped around his heart. They were face to face, looking deep into each other's eyes. Perhaps they would die there. George's only comfort was that if he did die

The Day that Grief Came to Stay

there he would at least see his Dad again. George felt like giving up. He'd had enough of struggling. George could feel himself falling asleep. All was quiet and very, very dark.

Then suddenly George could hear his Dad's voice cheering him on, "You can do it George. You can do anything!" All the times that Dad had taught George how to do stuff, like ride a bike and swim, came into his mind. Dad was egging him on and filling him with energy that fizzed through him like a glass of pop. George looked up and so did Grief. High above them a shaft of light had appeared. George began to climb out of the pit, one step at a time, a foot-hold here, a small space for his fingers there, slowly but surely, carrying Grief and determined to reach the top. It wasn't easy and it took a very long time but eventually he clambered to the very top of the pit and into the light, exhausted but exuberant. His Mum was waiting patiently at the top and wrapped George and Grief in a big blanket and took them home to bed.

George was allowed to stay off school for a while until he felt better. He had been through a lot and his whole world had changed but he was very slowly beginning to find a new *normal*.

One morning something strange happened. George was sat on the floor watching TV with Grief wrapped around his middle when suddenly George laughed at something on the TV. He had been distracted and had forgotten that Grief was there, he hadn't even been thinking about his Dad as much either. And then it happened, an actual out-loud *laugh*, George's very first since his Dad had died.

Suddenly, without any warning, Grief loosened his grip from around George's middle, reached out a pair of big feet, set them down and began to uncurl. His legs were like two strips of black liquorice and there was a big lump of fur at the top which unfolded to reveal a long, thin, furry body, two long liquorice-stick arms with big hands and long fingers. Finally, out popped a head with a plain, dark face, big furry ears, the saddest green eyes, no nose and a tiny mouth. Grief stared straight back at George and cleared his throat.

"Enjoy your programme," said Grief. George did and laughed some more. It felt good, but a bit wrong at the same time. Surely you weren't allowed to laugh if your Dad had died? But Grief kept giving him reassuring instructions.

"Play with your computer game," said Grief. "It helps take your mind off things," and he was right. It distracted George so that he didn't have to think about his Dad constantly.

The next day Grief said, "Go out and play with your friends," so George did and it was great to see them again. The day after that Grief said, "Watch your favourite TV shows," and George did and little by little he began to notice that he and Grief were spending less and less time together and that he was smiling and laughing more each day.

"It's OK to laugh and smile again," said Grief and George listened and nodded. He began to feel better and a little bit more like his old self, or was it his new self?

From that day on George and Grief saw less and less of each other until one day George noticed that Grief had moved out of the house entirely. However, Grief's visits would never stop, not even when George was a grown man. He would still appear, particularly on anniversaries, birthdays and holidays but sometimes he paid surprise visits, catching George completely unawares, always when he was missing his Dad the very most.

THE HOODIE

Gabrielle Pearson Heavisides

It was all scrunched up at the bottom of the wardrobe. Could you call it a wardrobe? It was a disgrace, he knew that. One door was wrenched off and nothing was actually hanging on the rail. The clothes were flung in – socks, boxers, t-shirts, jeans. Some were clean – well cleanish, others grubby, all crumpled and in need of a good shake before he could put them on.

Lately, he'd begun to notice he was outgrowing most of them – sleeves too short, trousers not quite at half mast, but definitely creeping up that way, t-shirts tight. He needed something bigger and that was why he had rummaged deeper down into the pile than normal. And that's why he had found it. It came as a shock. He brought it up to his face and buried his head in it. He was sure now. It was what he thought it was. There was no doubting it. It smelt of Craig even after all these years – his stale sweat, the hint of cigs and the Lynx deodorant. Craig had lived in this hoodie. He inhabited it like skin.

Carl would lie in bed watching him getting ready to go out. Craig would stand in front of the cracked wardrobe mirror waxing his hair and styling it deftly between his fingertips. He would have a quick sniff of his armpits before pulling on his hoodie and then he would turn round to Carl grinning, "How do I look?"

Carl had dreaded this moment. He would say, "Don't go. Please don't go" and Craig would laugh: "Don't worry. I'm very careful – just like a cat. I belong in the dark. Look."

Then he would pull his hoodie down over his face and slink around the room and Carl would cower under the blanket because he knew this always ended with a pounce and they would both roll over together and smother their laughter in the pillow. But Carl wasn't really laughing.

"OK. I'll see you later," Craig would say.

Then he would slide open the window and climb out on to the roof of the lean-to and drop to the ground. Carl would lower the window and before he pulled the curtains closed he would watch Craig running off, keeping into the shadows of the houses opposite. And sometime, hours later, he'd hear him climb back and in the morning when he was getting himself up for school, Craig would be bundled up in the bed opposite with his clothes scattered across the floor.

But one night he didn't come back. That whole day had seemed different. Craig had been on edge, constantly checking his mobile, receiving text messages, holding whispered conversations and ending them abruptly when Carl appeared. That evening he didn't hum to himself while he was getting ready to go out, no posing in front of the mirror and then turning with a cheeky grin for Carl to admire him. There was no prowling round the room pretending to be a cat, no stalking or pouncing or meowing in Carl's ear to make him laugh. Craig didn't bother to wax his hair or check he smelt good. But he did pull out a scarf and wound it round his neck and then experimented with pulling it over the lower half of his face and pulling his hoodie well down. Carl watched him from the bed and shuddered. Craig must have sensed something because he swung round.

"Got to take precautions tonight. It might get busy."

The Hoodie

Carl knew it was useless asking him not to go. Craig was buzzing. Nothing could hold him back now. Neither of them said anything. He watched Craig until he had disappeared and then lowered the window as he always did and got back into bed. He lay for a long time in the dark straining for any unusual sounds and occasionally he got up and peered through the curtains. He expected to see the night sky lit up with flames or the searchlights of the police helicopters or the sounds of sirens maybe or people running; but all was quiet. He wasn't reassured and he lay awake worrying for a long time. It seemed that the first half of the night he slept lightly with a series of dreams each one ending with a chase; but was it him being chased or Craig? He could never quite make out who the fugitive was, running through the shadows with his face covered. And then he fell into a heavy sleep and woke feeling drugged and sluggish in the early hours of the morning. He knew before he had even opened his eyes that Craig was not in the other bed. He was alone.

And he had not seen Craig since. He couldn't talk about how he felt. He got angry and smashed up the room again and again till all his energy was spent and hope faded. Then he had kept himself to himself. People knew to leave him alone. He was happy with that because he wanted to concentrate all his energies on not forgetting Craig. He filled much of his time by re-living everything he could remember about Craig. Those memories were all he had. Until now, until this moment, this discovery.

Carl stared at the hoodie in his hand. How could it be here? But it was. He could hear Craig as if he was back, here in the room with him. "How do I look?" It was glorious to hear that familiar voice again, the texture of it, the tenderness in it and the hint of a laugh curling up from underneath waiting to explode. He wanted to see him again, to feel him, to get inside his skin.

He knew what he had to do. He stood up and carefully drew the hoodie over his head feeling it settle on his frail shoulders and then he slid his arms into the sleeves. He stood in front of the wardrobe and admired himself in the mirror. He had grown into the hoodie. He understood another thing too, why Craig had loved it so much. It wasn't just the look of it. It was more than that. He felt secure inside it. The fleecy material warmed his bare skin. The hoodie did what no-one had ever done. He felt hugged. He pulled down the hood and he felt hidden, safe, invisible even. He walked towards the window and slid it open. It was dark now and he leaned out, measuring the distance down to the roof of the lean-to. He could already see himself melting into the shadows of the houses opposite. He was ready now.

But then there came another voice, a different memory. "Don't go. Please don't go."

He swung round and came face to face with the shrouded figure in the mirror. He had to decide. He knew that. He turned towards his bed and gave the answer he had so longed to hear all those years ago. "Don't worry. I'm sticking with you," he said.

Carl stepped away from the wardrobe and crossed over to the window. He slid it shut and closed the curtains. As he opened his bedroom door and stepped out into the light he could hear voices. He pushed back the hood from his face and walked downstairs.

MAGGOTY JOHNSON

Angela Topping

In Maggoty Woods it's dark and grim.
The worms crawl out and the worms crawl in.
Maggoty's buried six feet deep.
He rests his eyes but he's not asleep.

Maggoty Johnson loved to dance.
With his cap and bells, he used to prance
and caper up and down on stage.
Now he's at the skeleton age.

In Maggoty Woods there's no church near.
The ground's unholy, it's dark and drear.
Maggoty chose it specially
as the sort of place he'd like to be.

Maggoty Johnson was called Lord Flame.
Now he goes by a different name.
He haunts these woods and he haunts them well.
Sooner or later you'll be under his spell.

In Maggoty Woods it's dark and grim.
The worms crawl out and the worms crawl in.
Maggoty's buried six feet deep.
He rests his eyes but he's not asleep.

Note: Samuel Johnson (1691–1773) was Britain's last professional jester. He is buried in woodland near Gawsworth Hall, Cheshire, on Maggoty Lane. A legend says

Wordlife

that if you call his name thirteen times on Hallowe'en, he will rise up and perform for you. Everything in this poem is true.

PIED PIPER

Rachael Bate

When I was a very small child my granny would sit me on her knee and I would say: "Tell me the story, granny!"

I am sure you will know the story too: a mysterious stranger arrives in a town troubled by rats. He plays a lovely tune on his pipe and leads the rats away; but when the townspeople do not pay him he plays another enchantingly beautiful tune and the children of the town follow him. In the morning, they are nowhere to be seen, they have all disappeared. It is not a pleasant comfortable story: but all the best stories have scary bits.

The reason I liked it was for the mystery. Things do not just disappear: they can get lost, mislaid, forgotten or hidden but 'disappear' is just a word we use when we can no longer see them.

Once, I asked my granny: "Where did the children go?" And in return she asked me: "Where do you think they went?"

I thought for a moment: "I think they must have gone somewhere magical. The Piper was magical; he must have come from somewhere that was magical too." That made sense.

It was only after that summer holiday when I stayed with my granny, that I discovered the true meaning of adventures. It was certainly a magical summer, but as for happy endings? Long ago, I learnt there is no such thing as a truly happy ending. For everything you win, you lose something else and for every hero there is someone you will never see again.

It was also during those weeks that I discovered something about my granny, something that nobody else in the family knew. She had had an adventure of her own; many years ago when she was my age. She had done something amazing and so very brave and if she had not been as courageous as she was, so many things would have been different.

That first night after I got home from my holidays, I dreamt about my granny. She was a young girl again and she was running. There was the castle from the picture on my granny's wall. This castle was my home, or the nearest thing to it. I was not seeing the dream as you sometimes do when you sleep, like you are watching a film of someone else; I was that girl, I was my granny and I was holding the hand of a younger, smaller girl who was crying.

"It will be alright," I said to the little girl, "I will look after you. You must be very brave. Hold tight to my hand and follow me."

As we crossed the courtyard, I was intensely aware of my surroundings, the smell of damp honeysuckle, the long grey banners with their black symbols, cool evening air, the bark of a guard dog not far off. Had it caught our scent? Voices too, echoing in the gloom. Guards' voices, gruff and harsh.

"Where are we going?" asked the girl.

"An adventure," I replied, my voice low." Just you and me."

"Where to?" she asked, with interest.

"Just over here a bit further," I said, trying to keep the tone of my voice calm. Panic was one thing, but I did not want to get her too excited either.

"Through the castle gates!" gasped the little girl. "I've never been that far before! Out there it's another world!"

Pied Piper

"That is why it's an adventure," I said. "Hush now, we must be as quiet as mice."

We were leaving our world, a world that was at war, where there were those who wished us harm. They would soon be here and we could not wait for them to find us. We were leaving everything behind; our homes, our childhood, our families and friends, everything that made us who we were. It was scary to think of it so I just had to concentrate on our escape. The girl was a lot smaller than me, I had to look after her and keep her safe no matter what. It was my duty. No-one else could do it but me and nobody could help me either.

"Why is the sky that funny colour?" she asked.

"It is the sunset," I replied; although I knew that the sun had set hours ago and in the opposite direction. The reddish glow on the horizon came from many fires burning. Our fatherland was burning.

Then she called my name, as if to ask more questions but I shushed her again; she was making too much noise. Where we were going we had to make ourselves invisible; we had to melt into the shadows and the forgotten places. It would be far better if no-one noticed us at all because then there would be no difficult questions and no need to lie. I was not good at lying, I never had been.

We had only the clothes on our backs and one thing more: only the golden star on a chain the little girl wore could link us to the world we were leaving behind. It was a dangerous thing to have in our possession, but it was precious too, nearly as precious as the little girl herself.

The little girl who clung onto my hand kept looking up at me, in awe and wonder. She seemed to be expecting me to say something, to explain, to make her understand. I suppose to her I was a grown-up who would know what to do. I suddenly felt very afraid and my fear soon turned to panic and my heart began to race uncontrollably; a cold shiver shot through my body from my neck and down my spine. I had no idea what was waiting for us beyond the castle gates, there could be enemies there too and there would certainly be danger. All I knew was that it was a new world where all the old certainties would be gone. Would we ever return home? I did not know.

Dreams never end where you want them to. Bad dreams are always too long and good dreams are always too short.

Going home is sometimes hard. When you are somewhere new, with people who do not know you, you become a new person and that can be exciting as well as a little bit scary. I knew that even if I never saw the friends I had made that summer ever again, at least I had known them and they had known me. We had shared an adventure that would never be forgotten.

COUNTING MARBLES

Sheila Blackburn

Later, the snow came. Not the soft-dancing, flattering stuff of Christmas cards and winter-washed landscapes. This snow was ice-teeth sharp; it came prowling on the bitter jaws of a biting wind that howled and hunted in sorry-bleak places. Unwanted, uninvited, it pushed itself into Jez's little world, dirty-white, harsh, uncompromising.

He shuddered to his bones. His grimy red-raw fingers fidgeted at the broken zip of a thin jacket. He huddled further into the urine-stinking corner of the stairwell with its huge, threatening graffiti – scrunched himself against the awfulness of everything. All round, frowning tower-block fingers clawed at the hard sky as day turned to night, mean and grey. Lights pin-pricked the cold streets; a thousand eyes watching and blinking their contempt.

Hot tears on chapped cheeks. Jez pressed his face into the wet-cold knees of his tracksuit. The image of the big black car, slow-moving like a giant, ugly insect, was there again: taking Henson away ... Old Henson had truly gone. The one person he had trusted and respected, finished in a heart-stopping hammer-blow of pain. Jez flung his head back, raged at the hopelessness – roared until he was weak and the sound was just a desperate, hurting whimper.

"See if you need a marble for your 'happy-jar', now!" A final cry into the emptiness, then Jez laughed, exhausted, hysterical.

It would have been typical of the man to add a marble at this precise, desperate moment; Old Henson had always been able to see good in everything. In the middle of this nasty, vicious snow-storm, he would have been glad of his cosy flat. Another marble in the jar. Clunk.

As for this hard grief: "At least we knew each other for a while, lad." Clunk!

Old Henson had always helped kids, like Jez, who had grown up relying on his scalding-sweet tea and a safe, undemanding place to escape all the squalor and despair. He had invented the happy-jar for them, a reason to look beyond the awful-obvious and find something better – a little bit of hope.

"Always look on the bright side," Old Henson grinned. Hard to think of him any other way.

"Robin's been singing on the balcony today!" The sharp eyes glittered like the twinkling marble dropping into the happy-jar. Clunk!

Some of the other kids sneered, already weary-old, defeated by resignation and contempt. But Jez was fascinated. The shiny-smooth glass-ball rattled happily onto many others already in the jar. Old Henson could always find a reason to add marbles, seldom taking one out, through anger or sadness, as his rules dictated.

"Spring's here, lads," he waved at the daffodils struggling in his window-box. "Another marble, I reckon." Clunk.

"First swallows on the wires. Summer's on its way." Clunk.

And when the distant trees burned fire-bright away to the west, when rainbows shimmered or frost-patterns laced the inside of his windows, Old Henson and his marbles chuckled happily.

Clunk. Clunk. And clunk again.

Counting Marbles

Now, twisted and choking with huge grief, Jez lifted his face to the stinging snow and heard the sound of the marbles falling and freeing all the memories ... Old Henson's advice, given simply, taken seriously. Small-steps, bits of progress, fragments of unremarkable things – he made them all remarkable little celebrations by another clattering marble.

With a mother distracted by cheap booze and hopeless boyfriends, Jez only had Old Henson to listen and share – a goal well-scored, a lesson learned, a friendship forged. The marbles rattled and clunked into the jar.

"How many, do you think?"

"Never enough, lad."

"What'll you do when it's full?"

"Get another." It was simple. Jez thought that Old Henson must have a cupboard full of jars, each filled to the brim and twinkling with happiness.

Sometimes, the reason for another happy-marble was hard to understand. Like the time Jez befriended a new boy. Old Henson was ready with a marble, rolling it between leather-tough fingers.

"Another?" Jez was incredulous. "Mrs Ermington-Trott's put her Rupert in our dump-school to *widen his experiences* ... Poor bugger! What's good about that?"

"You chose to be his mate an' help him ... Nobody else bothered. *That's* worth a marble ..."

Old Henson shifted against the rusting balcony rails, scratched his nose and looked down at all the cratered-concrete far below. He knew about folks who wanted to *make a difference* – just daft, interfering questions and dream-empty plans and useless publicity.

The lads' unlikely friendship had ended as suddenly as it had begun – quite simply, Rupert hadn't been able to cope. After less than half a term, he convinced his mother he'd learned enough then returned to an expensive boarding school, boasting of his 'achievements'.

"They were kind to me." Jez tried to save something from the experience.

"Showed me things can be better – not like all this." He clenched his fists against the frowning tower-blocks, and black-burned cars and all the graffiti.

"Different – but not *always* better," Old Henson was purposefully sharp.

"Wherever we are, it's what we make of it. An' now, *you* have a choice, lad. You've seen different ways. So – you might do nothin' – like the rest of 'em – an' stay hereabouts forever. Or – you can take chances an' make somethin' of yourself."

Jez looked at him intently.

"Mrs E-T – she didn't know, but she gave you that choice – an' that's worth another marble, for sure." Clunk!

It might have been a turning point, the start of something big, that particular marble. Jez wanted to hear more. But then came the blue flashing lights cutting into the darkness. It was the last marble the old man put into the happy-jar.

There had never been anyone like Old Henson, with his knowing smile and his easy-wisdom, his patient wife and their cluttered flat.

"You – you're just like me, lad," he'd say, grinning. "You understand. You know the need for the marbles."

But now he had gone. And in the bitter snow and all the raw space left behind, only one thing was important: the happy-jar and all its marbles.

The snow-slaps stung harder than before and the wet-cold track-suit plastered heavily against his legs. Jez pulled again at his thin jacket and heard the sound of his own

Counting Marbles

sobbing, louder than all the marbles clinking. He pushed dirty knuckles against his eyes, swallowed hard and finally shuffled from the hiding place. Too tired to use the stairs, he leaned against a stained wall and jabbed at the lift-call button. Somewhere below, the lift groaned at the prospect of another journey. Its doors shut against the night-town and imprisoned Jez amongst peeling posters and crude felt-tip scribbles; he folded his arms and felt only slightly more determined.

The Hensons' door was always off the catch. Jez pressed the bell and walked inside. At the end of the short, dark corridor, he stood framed in a doorway, waiting with a thin-lipped frown. No words. He had no words. His hood slipped off, his hair stuck up awkwardly. He kicked at the thread-bare carpet and the soles of his trainers flapped like gossiping tongues.

Some other kids were here again. As if nothing had happened. Empty eyes regarded him. Nobody spoke. He didn't blame them. They thought he was different – not better, or worse, just different. They weren't here out of respect for Old Henson, or sadness. They were here as ever, for a hot drink and a quiet place. Like so much sad, worthless lost property in an abandoned place. They didn't understand the marbles and they didn't understand Jez and his odd friendships. He leaned against the door frame and waited.

Eventually, old Ma Henson looked up: "You're back, son. Good. Kettle's on." Jez moved to the little kitchen, grateful for some things staying the same when so much was changing. He stirred two sugars into strong tea and stood watching it swirl round the cracked mug. There was a scuffle and old Ma Henson was at his side. Jez looked into her lined face; she sighed, long and weary-sad and there was no need to say anything. The silence stood between them, strangely comforting. Then, very slowly and deliberately, she held out her hand. A shiny black marble winked up at him. She knew! She understood.

"You'll have to give me a good reason to add this to the jar," she said, testing him.

Outside, the snow prowled and whined. Carefully, deliberately, Jez lifted the happy-jar off its shelf. All the bright marbles shifted and twinkled at each other, excited, waiting for him.

"I'd say it's good to be cosy and safe in here tonight."

She nodded. And Jez let the marble fall into the jar with a clunk that was full of hope and reassurance.

DEADLY DANCING

Hilary Bowen

Not everyone had a sister as horrible as Daisy-Jo Whittle. If being horrible was an Olympic event, Daisy-Jo mightn't actually qualify, but she *would* mug the winners and steal their medals. She was the reason Jack was currently thigh-high in weeds on the wrong side of a cemetery gate. He looked back. Five girls jogged to the bars and parted to let his horrible sister through.

"Come out," she said.

"No."

"Then we'll come in."

"In there? No way: new blouse!" objected Panda-Eyes (the girl on Daisy-Jo's right with an overdose of mascara).

"I've just had my nails done!" said Horse-Teeth. "I'm not climbing a rusty old gate!"

Daisy-Jo looked like she'd swallowed a slug. "We can wait," she sneered through the bars. "Enjoy being locked in with the ghosts, squirt. Don't get eaten!"

Jack leaned against a wall and watched them slouch away (although, knowing his horrible sister, she wouldn't go far). Eaten? As if! "That's zombies, stupid! Anyway, there are worse things than ghosts."

"Very glad to hear you say so!" said the ghost, right by his ear.

Jack turned, swallowing. "You're ... dead?"

"What gave it away? The see-through skin? The hollow voice? The fact that you put your elbow straight through me when you leaned against my crypt?"

"Err ... no," said Jack. "'twas the hat. Nobody wears top hats any more unless they're ... "

" ... dead." The ghost slumped. "Excellent. Not only am I deceased, but I'm unfashionably so."

Jack knew he should be scared. But, frankly, with a sister as horrible as Daisy-Jo, there was no fear room left for some poor old dead chap. Besides, he looked quite nice. His wrinkles were crinkly and cheerful. His moustache looked like it had come straight out of a joke shop, complete with glasses and false nose. He had kindly blue eyes and a mouth that turned up at the corners. Then there was the penguin suit and bow-tie. In Jack's experience, bow-ties weren't worn by supervillains or monsters, but by clowns and, occasionally, snooker players. Neither of which sounded too terrible.

"So – who are you? What are you doing here?"

"My name is Mr Stipps. As for what I am doing, I might well ask you the same thing." The ghost raised bushy eyebrows. "I, at least, belong here."

"Trying to avoid my sister. I'm stuck here until she goes away."

"Ahh. Then perhaps you can help me."

"Help you?" Jack looked around nervously. "How?"

The ghost hesitated. "I want to become a skeleton," he said at last.

Jack began to laugh, then realised that would be rude and turned it into a cough. "Um ... "

"I suppose you're wondering why."

Jack nodded.

"I want to dance."

Looking around, Jack was expecting the camera crew to step into view and announce that he'd been Pranked, or Jackass-ed. They stubbornly failed to appear. "Uhh ... what?"

Mr Stipps sighed. "Every Friday night, the skeletons dance in the graveyard. It's their thing. All I can do is watch,

Deadly Dancing

because I have no body." He sighed again. "I used to love to dance."

Every Friday night? Real skeletons? Jack wondered what sort of dancing they did. Something old-fashioned maybe, with bowing and curtseying. Or tap dancing. They wouldn't even need the shoes! He vowed to come one night and find out.

The ghost harrumphed.

"Oh. Yeah. Sorry," said Jack. "Look – I'd like to help. Really. But I don't know anything about becoming a skeleton."

"You just have to find the right bones." Jack took a step back, and Stipps waved his arms. "No, no. No grave-robbing or anything like that. It's all very tasteful, I assure you. My body is stored right here, in my ancestral crypt. Look, I'll show you. Reach under that rock. No, *that* one."

Jack bent to the stone by the crypt, and tugged it from the weeds. It was surprisingly light.

"Garden ornament," said Mr Stipps. "It's hollow. There's a key inside. And a torch." Jack noticed the key was made of bone. He hoped it didn't belong to any of the residents.

"Follow me." Stipps vanished through the solid wooden doors. Jack hesitated. What was the worst that could happen? Being locked in a square stone vault until he starved and his bones crumbled? Or leaving the cemetery and facing his horrible sister? It was no contest. He unlocked the door. Stone steps descended into the dark. The torch lit them with a dim but steady beam.

"Don't dawdle!"

"I'm not dawdling." Jack broke out of his dawdle and rejoined the ghost at the bottom of the stairs.

"They're in here." Mr Stipps gestured toward the narrow corridor ahead, lined with doorways on either side. "I just don't know where."

Stepping forward, Jack immediately saw the problem. In the first room, all the bones were long and thin. Leg bones, if he was any judge. The opposite room had fingers, the one after that, ribs. "Don't you *know* which ones are yours?"

"No."

"Aren't they labelled?"

The ghost spread his arms. Jack could see the grimy brickwork through them. "Of course. Perhaps I should look for the ones with 'Horatio Stipps' carved in bright gilt lettering, hmm?"

"I was only trying to help," muttered Jack. "What do you want from me?"

"I want you to *think*!" Mr Stipps looked deflated. "I hoped ... perhaps ... you could bring new perspective to my dilemma."

New *what* to his *what*? Jack frowned as his brain ran and hid from the unfamiliar words. As it fled, it passed a lightbulb and set it off in his head.

"I've got it!"

"Got what?" asked the ghost.

"I know how to find your bones," said Jack. "The skeletons in the graveyard."

"What about them?"

"Well, they must have been ghosts once. Some of them, anyway." Jack hopped from foot to foot. "They worked out how to find *their* bones. Why don't you just ask one of them?"

"Because ... well, obviously because ... I mean ... " There was a long pause. "You know, boy, you might be onto something. I don't suppose ... you could ask them?"

Deadly Dancing

Jack thought that, if Mr Stipps wanted his bones back so badly, he should do some of the work himself. However, it's never wise to quarrel with someone who could haunt your bedsheets for the rest of eternity. He decided to compromise.

"We'll both go."

Minutes later, they knocked on the ornate wooden door of another mausoleum. It swung open, revealing the figure behind it.

"Young Stipps. And a living boy?" The skeleton grinned, having little choice in the matter. "I hope this is important. You interrupted my meditation."

Jack couldn't stop himself. "Meditation?"

"Indeed. With the right spiritual energies and emanations, I opine that it will be possible for me to move up the evolutionary chain." Jack's face must have looked as blank as he felt, because the skeleton tapped its foot and sighed. "I hope to grow flesh."

"You want to *live* again?!"

"That, alas, is impossible. Death is irreversible. Flesh, however, is not."

"So ... like ... a zombie?"

"The possibilities are endless." The skeleton glared. "Why, with flesh, I could go anywhere! Jamaica ... Bournemouth ... Florida ... "

Jack had been to Florida last year. Daisy-Jo pushed him out of the log-flume in Disneyworld. He'd nearly drowned. "Florida?"

"Retirement villages," answered the skeleton, dreamily. "We fit right in."

Stipps cleared his throat, in clear meaning.

"It is important, actually," Jack said, hastily. "We were wondering. How did you find your bones, to become a skeleton?"

"I just went and chose them"

"Yes – but how did you know they were your bones?"

The skeleton's shoulder bones clicked as it shrugged. "I didn't. I just chose ones that would fit, that's all. It's what's *inside* that counts, you know."

"It's what's inside that counts ... " breathed Mr Stipps, a look of ecstasy on his face. He glided away, leaving the skeleton to lecture empty air about poor manners today. "Thank you, m'boy!"

The last thing Jack heard, as he left the cemetery, was Stipps's voice floating after him. "Now to find a good pair of dancing knees." Jack grinned, feeling really good about his evening. The feeling evaporated as Daisy-Jo and her gang surrounded him.

"You're gonna pay for running away, squirt!"

The gang had a variety of games they liked to play with Jack. For example, there was 'Chase Jack onto the gravel then steal his shoes', and 'Throw Jack into the duck pond'. Tonight's game was 'Spin Jack around repeatedly until he's sick'.

They whirled him, screaming in glee, and then screaming in earnest as a skeleton in a top hat clambered over the graveyard gates.

"You like to spin, hmm?" said Mr Stipps. He bowed to Daisy-Jo, and Jack was dumped on the ground as the skeleton sailed into the air with her, careening around in a wild, aerial waltz. Her face went white, then green, her screams became moans and moments later, her supper left her body. Jack scrambled out of the way. The gang of girls was not so quick as first the gunk, then Daisy-Jo landed on their heads. They collapsed in shrieking outrage.

Deadly Dancing

"Run, m'boy," suggested Mr Stipps. Jack did, grinning as he thought of that stinky mess pouring forth from Daisy-Jo's pretty little mouth. As he headed home, he held onto one triumphant thought.

"Maybe it really is what's inside that counts!"

THE DOG-FATHER

Catherine Bruton

My dad gave me Lottie just before he went on tour. 'On tour' makes him sound like some kind of pop star, playing sell-out gigs around the world. But he's not: he's in the army and 'on tour' just means he's going to fight in a warzone somewhere. This time it was Helmand, which, in case you don't know, is in Afghanistan, and is properly dangerous.

Dad told me not to cry when he left. He said I should look after Mum. And he gave me Lottie.

Lottie was only a puppy: twelve weeks old, soft fluffy fur, big eyes and big feet. Dad said that when he came back from tour we'd enter her into one of those TV talent shows. He and I had watched this one with a dog who could sing along to the 'Coronation Street' theme tune and we'd both laughed so much Mum said we'd do ourselves an injury. Dad reckoned Lottie could do way better than that. "Lottie's not just any old dog," he said. "She's the Dog-father!"

After Dad left I started teaching Lottie tricks every day after school. After my dad went on tour I stopped hanging out with the other kids on the base, because it seemed like all they played was war games and pretending to be soldiers getting their legs shot off, or blinded (like what happened to Kyle Winstanley's dad) or killed by a roadside bomb: the stuff I dream about every night when my dad is away.

So I hang out with Lottie instead. And I teach her tricks.

***

The Dog-father

"What can it do then?" I was sitting in the big waiting room, staring at the swirly carpet, wondering what my mum was going to do when she found out. Then I looked up and saw this little girl staring at me. She was about six years old, wearing a cheerleader's costume and loads of make-up, and she had her hair pulled back into a pony tail so tight it made her eyes turn up at the ends.

"Your dog, what can it do?" she repeated, hands on hips.

"She dances," I said.

"Cool! So do I!" she said, producing one of those baton thingies that was about five times as big as she was and twirled it round and round so fast I thought she was going to take her false eyelashes out.

I looked round at all the other contestants waiting to perform. There were singing grannies, middle-aged magicians, dancing troupes, kids in top hats and tap-shoes, teenagers practising magic tricks with their grand-dads. All of them seemed way more talented than me and Lottie.

"Where's your mam and dad?" said the twirlie baton girl.

"They couldn't come."

"Show us what she can do then."

She nodded at Lottie who stared up at me, mournfully. She was tired. It had taken us much longer than I expected to get here and we'd got lost and had to walk for ages. And I'd left my sandwiches on the bus. So we were both hungry.

"I'm gonna wait till we get on stage," I said.

"Suit yourself!" said the baton girl and she went off to practise twirling her baton some more.

I stroked Lottie's soft ears and said, "Not much longer, girl."

Wordlife

Lottie looked up at me with her big chocolate button eyes and whimpered quietly. Only I was wrong. It was hours before we got to go on stage. I fell asleep in the waiting room and woke up to a woman shaking me and saying. "Where are your parents, sonny?"

"Oh they just went out to get summat to eat," I lied. "They'll be back soon."

***

Turns out Lottie gets stage fright. When we went out under all the hot yellow lights, Lottie started to whimper loudly. Which was how I felt too. But I reminded her, "We're doing this for Dad, Lottie. Remember?"

"And why are you here today, Joe and Lottie?" asked the nice judge with the twinkly eyes and the big smile.

"My dad wanted me to teach her tricks," I said.

"And is your dad with you?" asked the scary judge. The one who tells people they're rubbish. Even nine year olds with dogs.

"No, I said, 'He's —"

Only I never got to tell them where my dad was because that was when the police turned up.

***

You don't usually get police turning up to talent shows so it caused a bit of a stir. Especially when it turned out they were looking for me.

"Your mam is frantic with worry, son," said the big burly police officer with the red cheeks.

"How did she know he was here?" asked the twinkly-eyed judge.

The Dog-father

"Something about a promise he made his dad," said the police officer.

Lottie whimpered then, when he mentioned Dad. And I blinked really, really hard because I didn't want to cry.

The police officer explained everything to the judges. About the road-side bomb, and how they'd flown my dad home and how they thought for a while that he might make it. And how, in the end, he didn't.

And about half an hour later my mum turned up. And she hugged me and said, "I hope you weren't going to start without me!" And Lottie perked up because the competition people had found some dog biscuits.

When we went on and did our act, she was amazing. She did all the tricks perfectly. No mistakes. Afterwards, the audience cheered and cheered, and the twinkly-faced judge said that Lottie was a doggy superstar and the scary judge told me my dad would be proud of both of us. And Lottie wagged her tail and yapped and that made the audience cheer even more.

She fell asleep in the car on the way home and so did I. And I didn't dream of guns and war and roadside bombs. I dreamt about me and my dad and Lottie. Doing doggy tricks and laughing – till we did ourselves an injury.

THE WIZARDS' TEA SHOP

Pat Davies

Annie loved the old shop. The windows were grimy and behind the glass were net curtains that looked as if they had not been washed in many years, but to Annie the shop was a magical place. She had never seen anywhere quite like it. The windows stuck out onto the pavement, narrow and almost semi-circular, as if made for tiny mannequins or stands for extravagant feather-covered hats. The door was wide and wooden, and had three semi-circular steps leading to it. It was blue and faded and old.

It was winter and all Annie's family was walking from the bus stop towards the little shop. Something went wrong with Archie's pram. As her mother and father bent down, trying to loosen the old plastic bag that was wound round the wheels, Annie skipped on, knowing that the delay would give her more time outside the little shop. She loved standing there imagining what had been inside. She had many theories. It might have been a wonderful shop where you could buy any fancy dress costume and become a queen, a spaceman or a pirate, a flower shop that was a little like a tropical jungle on the inside, with snakes and tropical birds amongst the greenery, or a shop full of old-fashioned toys like the ones she had seen on television, with automated dolls playing the piano and wonderful tin robots and puppets that came alive once the lights went out and the shop closed. She was thinking of all these things, her cheeks red from the icy weather, when she saw something very unusual. The dirty net curtain twitched a little as if someone was inside. She thought she saw a glimpse of a pair of twinkling blue eyes, a thin face and long, white hair.

The Wizards' Tea Shop

Annie was fascinated. She ran to the window and pressed her nose against the freezing glass. As she did so, the wide door opened with a slight creak. Annie did not know what to do. Her parents were very strict about her going off alone. She stood at the bottom of the steps and suddenly the old door swung open.

The scene that greeted her took her breath away. In all her wildest dreams she had never imagined this. In the little shop there seemed to be a ridiculous number of round tables jostling for space. There was a thin, tall, wiry woman threading her way through the tables, tray held high, serving tea and cakes to men who looked like they'd stepped straight out of a fairy tale. There were tall, thin ones and short, stout ones. Some wore tall hats decorated with stars and magical symbols and some were bald with long plaited beards and oriental robes. They all sat at tables covered with red and white checked tablecloths. The noise they made was tremendous as they shouted for the waitress, who now seemed to be carrying two trays aloft. When they were not shouting to the waitress, they all seemed to be shouting to each other across the little room. She could not believe she had not heard the noise from outside.

"Wizards!" Annie thought to herself. "Very noisy wizards!"

As she looked round in amazement, she saw the cheery face she'd glimpsed behind the curtain. There was an empty seat next to him, and he crooked his finger in her direction. She squeezed through, between the tables, almost colliding with the waitress, who tutted at her and swerved into an impossibly tiny space to let her past. She felt very small amongst the wizards at the table. Next to her sat a thin man dressed in black who wore a top hat. She did not look too closely at his hair, which looked a little like many thin snakes, curling this way and that. The other occupant of the table was a small man with a big smile who was dressed in a moss-green suit with a red waistcoat and a big gold pocket watch. He did not look too much like a wizard, but when he passed her a plate full of biscuits they changed into big gold coins as she looked at them. The tall, thin wizard who had opened the door to her looked sternly at the little man in the green suit. As he was doing so, Annie slipped one of the coins into her pocket, just as the little man waved his hands and the coins turned back into biscuits again. The man dressed in black poured her a cup of tea. She squealed as a black spider scurried across the table with a sugar cube on its back and waited patiently for her to take it. She took it from the spider and the creature scurried off, back behind the sugar bowl.

"I can't stay too long," Annie said, sadly. "My family will be looking for me."

The tall wizard said kindly, but loudly, making himself heard above the din, "You can be sure that when you leave here it will be as if no time has passed. Please stay for a little while. We have so few visitors who are not of our own type and, as you can see, wizards can be a little tiresome at times."

When he had finished speaking he passed her the largest piece of chocolate cake she had ever seen, and his eyes twinkled under his thatch of thick white hair. When the only thing left at the table were crumbs, a few sugar cubes and tea leaves, Annie got up from the little chair.

"Thank you for having me," she said politely.

The wizards all stood and bowed in her direction, and the wizard with the white beard guided her through the busy tea room to the door.

"Thank you for coming," he replied, smiling.

The Wizards' Tea Shop

Then, before she knew it, she was out in the cold street, and the shop again looked dirty and old. There was no noise that suggested the busy, noisy scene she had recently been part of.

"Did I imagine it?" she asked herself.

Then she felt something in her pocket. Her fingers closed round the big gold coin and she began laughing to herself as she skipped up the road to rejoin her family. She would never forget the day she got to take tea and cake with the wizards in the little tea shop behind the faded blue door.

GOING FOR GOLD

Derek Matthews

A goldfish bowl on a windowsill
Overlooked the stream,
And through a window, opened wide,
The goldfish eyed the scene.

She swam around to gather speed
And with a mighty jump,
She sailed on high into the sky
To land: kerslap! Sla ... bump!

She slithered down a muddy bank
And joined the water's flow,
Then dived, with happy gulps of joy,
To freedom down below.

She raced the rapids of the stream
In streaks of golden light
And drifted in a quiet lake
Of silver starlit night.

When morning came she flipped her tail
To face a golden day,
And, with new friends, she swirled along
And boldly zoomed away.

COLOUR CODING

Jo Mayers

On an odd day, someone might ask
What is your favourite colour?
It's OK to wonder what that question means. It's a confusing one.
It feels as though the answer will tell people something. Something important.
Perhaps it will.
Here is what I know:

When I am safe, I like
things to be yellow.
    The clever and friendly heads of
    daffodils in early spring.
        Or sweet, carefully smoothed
        lemon curd on warm bread.
            A golden-edged feeling
            of home. I like that.

When I feel sad,
I go out of my way
to look for red.
    The shout of a
    crimson scarf, streaming
    bannerlike in the air.
        Also the horror of
        hot embers, or a bead
        of warm blood.
            These are points.
            But they are not
            answers. They are tough.

Wordlife

Now. If I am delighted, I desire blue.
    Cornflowers scattered like dust specks
    across a cool meadow.
        And the eyes of the husky dog
        from across the street.
             Brave, deep things.
             A courage colour
             to look into. So these things
             are shards. They break through.

When I am asleep,
or in that strange
plodding state
just before waking,
I often see purple.
    The outer edges of sunsets,
    where night meets light
    in an indigo dream.
        Or the shade of a gorgeous plum,
        bristling like a two day bruise
        with juice, and fullness.
            My sleep visions never taste.
            Instead they dance, hovering
            over my closed eyes like violet space.

Jewel green is for fear.
It courses across grassy spaces,
crossing light with shadow
until the place between
becomes unclear.
    Emerald ink for frantic days,
    escaping my pen and making

Colour Coding

huge, looping forays onto the paper.
How close,
how dear to me this
lively life-blood. Leaf-coloured.

When energy flows,
and my limbs feel strong,
the only sight in mind is grey.
Not middling dishwater grey,
but that of sharp, towering
clouds on a stormy day.
Or the smooth centuries on
the surface of a stone,
worn and beaten yet somehow
light, perfect in the palm.
This sort of grey is old without ageing.
It can lift sad bones.

What can you see?
Look at this page
without using those little cells
at the back of your eye.
Do colours spring?
Can you see lights carouse
and swirl beyond your sight?
If not, not to fret.
It'll happen when you
only half expect.

EXAM ROOM

Don Nixon

We hunch tense at desks, spaced in guardsman ranks,
like athletes crouching for the starter's gun.
For good or ill, all preparation's done.
"You may begin." The form teacher's voice cranks
our tight wound limbs into chair creaking play.
I turn the paper, scan the question sheet.
My favourite's not come up. I feel the heat
of disappointment – then I spot a way.
I've revised that one, I can wing the rest.
I scroll down my mind screen. I start to write
and try to ease my pen, my knuckle white.
One question's done. The next a harder test.
Then utter panic. When I sneak a look,
my neighbour's on his second answer book.

FROZEN

Paul Palmer

I don't remember dying. Not the moment. I do remember the car. Red. It was dark. I remember cold, wet rain. Raindrops on my face. Raindrops and tears. But not *my* tears. Then a pause and lots of lights.

I remember moving. No. *Being* moved. Then everyone stopping. Standing back. Staring down at me; down at me and at each other. But there's nobody I recognise. So why do they look so sad? Then darkness ...

Now I'm ... here. Here? Everywhere. Nowhere. I'm home but it's not really my home anymore. Like visiting an old school. Once very familiar but now no longer part of you. Just a memory.

And the days, they blend into one another. Like a long summer holiday. Days without content or meaning. Each one uncounted. As one day ends another starts without thought or effort or attention. A twin. And the day after that. Another. Exactly the same again. If I concentrate *really* hard I could separate them but there seems little point.

So I'm back home. Home with my family. But not. I'm there but disconnected. I try to reach them but I can't.

So what *am* I now? To them, I mean. To my parents. I've become the empty chair. The picture on the wall. The snapshot memory staring at them. Smiling but static and frozen in time. Frozen in a moment: a much happier moment.

And mum and dad? Frozen too. But in a different moment. Their worst moment. They don't cry. Not properly. Certainly not as much as I thought they would. It's like they can't find their grief because they haven't found me yet.

They look for me. They stare at the things I've left behind. Looking for me in a possession. But they're just things. They're not me.

And in this moment, this frozen moment, I realise that for them my clutter has become me. I've become the trivia I left behind. The rubbish and junk transformed into everything I was. Debris becoming treasure. I'm the Everton mug on the kitchen work surface. I'm the coat on the back of my chair. I'm the dirty washing on my bedroom floor. I'm the sweet wrappers under my bed. I'm the smelly trainers. I'm the broken promise to take back a library book. To empty a bin. To clean my room.

All my imperfections made perfect and untouchable and noble and pure. Chores, left selfishly incomplete and ignored, become a way of holding onto me. A line straight back to me. Their *only* way back to me.

But that's just it. I wasn't perfect! They knew that! They told me often enough! I didn't help around the house. I never put my dirty washing in the basket. I'd sulk if I didn't get my way. The coat's only on the back of the chair because I never hung it up like I was asked. I argued. I whinged. I pouted. About stuff that didn't matter. And my rubbish, my stuff ... *this is* what they hold on to?

So they move nothing. For days they stumble upon piece after piece of clutter. Picking their way around these traces of me. Frozen. And so I'm frozen with them. Unable to move, too. Held by my shadows.

And now? They sit and hold hands. Wet eyed. Not crying. Quietly sharing the TV. It's on but they're not watching. It's just light and noise and distraction. Filling a gap. Until a film. And then ... a memory.

Frozen

Of an argument. A stupid argument. About choices. A TV remote. And *this* film. An argument over 90 minutes of our lives. I lost. I sulked. I was told off. I made mum a cup of tea. I made terrible cups of tea. *She* drank it though. She hated the tea. I hated the film. But we sat there. Sitting together. Making up in the slow deliberate silence and shared stubbornness.

And in a moment I've found my way back and I'm there! They've found me! No longer perfect. But selfish and considerate. Annoying and kind. Funny. Thoughtless, lazy and loving. And sorry. No longer *what* I left behind but *who* I left behind.

Tears flow. Full wet tears. Their tears. My tears. Shared relief. But then I feel something else. Something more.

The memory of stubbornness. The cold, weak cup of tea. Is that laughter? Yes. Quietly. Guiltily. Nervously. Underneath the tears at first. Then on top of them. Then wrapped around the grief. Circling it. Supporting it. Opposites. Working together. Healing.

And their laughter pulls me in even further. With them. Mum and dad and me. Holding each other. Sharing each other. The tears still there. Still full of sadness but no longer cold. No longer frozen in a moment, but warm and fluid like their memories of me. And suddenly, through them and their grief and their laughter, I feel alive!

SCARCE

Tanya D. Ravenswater

On a still night late in spring they came, drawn by the flickering light. Three figures: a boy, a mother and a father. Faces and hands pale as weathered bone. Travelling unburdened to the sandstone village: to the broken-hearted house, empty for so many years.

Only the old neighbour Thom, half-blind, knew they'd come. He sensed their presence, half-saw them from behind his moth-mouthed curtain. Gripping the sill, craving the cool, dark silence, he wondered if they were looking for him.

Thom followed their shapes moving down the drive, shifting around and about each other; a triangle of skirt; blurred grey coats swept stones, long mossed over. There were noises in the porch next door, light as leaves lapping or lost papers fluttering in the wind. A key coaxed the lock. The front door closed gently. Then, on the other side of the wall, he heard soft footfall everywhere on bare boards, muffled only by dust.

In another time, a distant life but the same place, Thom and Em were young. Em, now long gone smelled of beeswax, English lavender and honey. His beautiful, clever wife, sweet Em. Back then the house next door – the abandoned house that the whisperers of the village said was haunted – was a home to another family. Thom and Em had known Arthur and Rose and the little 'un, Jack. Jack who couldn't breathe when he ran. Little Jack, who died in bed one still night, late in spring. Jack died from nothing more, from nothing less, than not breathing. That was then.

Scarce

The strange family settled in, said the voices of the village. Though not in the way other families did. No furniture arrived. No new curtains or carpets. No television or any other kind of screen. They had no Xboxes, computers, fridges or washing machines. The plumber and electrician were asked to simply rewire and repair. There was hardly anything in there, the men said. Torn rags and dusters. Only newspapers on the floors, some pinned up at the windows. They did see stacks of the kind of cardboard trays farmers have, for eggs. Their questions about surnames, "Mr ... ?" and "Mrs ... ?" hung in the air, unanswered. Payment was received in cash, in crumpled notes palmed, unfolded.

No friends, grandparents or other family were invited in, the voices of the village observed. It took all sorts to make a world. What did these people do? Were they Eastern European? Italian? Irish? Travellers? Had they escaped some foreign prison? Whatever the case, they didn't fit in.

The mother and father usually remained, it seemed, about the house. They cleaned the windows, dusted the shadeless bulbs, arms rising, falling, frayed cloths circling. During the day they were occasionally seen on a woodland path or lingering, with their eyes closed, at the edge of a field, as if asleep on their feet. They would sometimes rest by a wall, scarcely noticeable.

The boy appeared at the village school.

"Although he's only joining us for a term, I'm sure we'll make him welcome," the teacher encouraged the class. "Tell everyone your name."

"Scarce." His voice was less than a whisper, for lip-reading more than for listening.

"Scarce who? Or ... who Scarce?" wondered the teacher.

"No other name. No need," mouthed the boy.

"No mates, more like!" laughed a hissing lad, behind his hand.

Scarce turned towards him his whole body trembling, but not with fear. He looked at the lad, his wide dark eyes blinking, saying nothing. Simply absorbing. A vibration, like a shiver only warmer, passed through the classroom.

When it came to maths, Scarce didn't make sense. He scrawled half-formed random numbers, always the wrong ones. He never put his hand up to answer questions. The teacher didn't push him. The family were only passing through. Regarding results and exams, "No need", the parents had whispered.

However, Scarce did like books. He pored over them, his lips brushing the pages.

"It's like he wants to eat them," a girl described. "He's smelling them first. The way you smell sweets, or a cone of chips, before you get dug in."

Another girl, famous for her imagination, said that she'd caught Scarce, licking a page with the strangest tongue she'd ever seen.

"It sort of quickly flicked out and in. Curled back up again, like a roll of liquorice, rewinding."

At break times the children studied Scarce, fluttering around the playground. His finger-tips often trailed the railings. He seemed lost, in his own mind-world. He wasn't like them. He didn't ask anything, didn't need friends. He didn't chat or play games like guns or football or catch. And there were those times, when he would lie motionless, face down on the stones.

"Too many late nights, watching television!" the teacher would say, making excuses for him.

"He doesn't have one!" replied the children. "He's just mad!"

Scarce

"We're all different," said the teacher. "Live and let live."

"Yes!" laughed the hissing lad. "But he's just like a crazy creature, playing dead!"

At night, next door, old Thom heard the mother and father, cleaning, sweeping, running water. From the room upstairs, where the light had flickered all those years – light, dark, dark, light – Thom heard hushed noises that went on for hours. Feet pattering, soft thuds against the walls. A low humming, a wordless singing, like a finger tracing the circumference of an empty jam jar.

As time went on the village children grew closer to Scarce. For reasons they couldn't quite explain, he allowed them to be themselves. Emily, missing her Mum, sat with him on the warm stones and stroked the drying wings of his damp grey coat. Afterwards on her hands, she noticed the slightest sheen, a powdering of silvery-gold.

"Just minerals. Mica perhaps, off the stones. Nothing unusual," said the hissing lad. Still, he noticed the same glistening dust on his arm, after Scarce bumped into him. He felt calmer later, hissed less. He didn't mind when the boy accidentally flew into him again.

That evening when the lad spoke to his father, he was told that trails of a bright substance had been found around the village pavements. Everyone was talking and joking about it, which made the atmosphere better, friendlier. But it wasn't mica. Under a microscope the lad and his father saw particles of what looked like pale shell or scales.

On a warm night, late in summer, a wind began to blow. Gently at first, wafting the willows into a swaying dance. Soon blowing more strongly, fanning everything outside into a fast rise and fall, as if under the winnowing wings of some invisible powerful beast. Old Thom, as he lay in bed, recalled how a long time ago, with his regiment in the desert, he had witnessed a sand storm. Never the like, not until this one. The windows of his house and the house next door shuddered and rattled. Dust lifted and blew in, clouds spun and swirled around the rooms. Thom shut his eyes, felt polishing grains against his cheeks. He remembered – or was it that he actually heard – the low humming, the wordless singing, like a finger following the rim of a glass, from the pale boy's room?

The storm died quickly. Against the stillness, at Thom's half-open window, there was a quiet, insistent tapping.

"Thom! Thom?" The voice so familiar, the scent, unmistakeable, of English lavender. Thom had never moved so quickly, had never seen so clearly. Outside, he saw his beautiful Em, smiling, waving up. Beside her, nose-end dusted with pollen, Little Jack. Thom sighed, laughed a little and waved back. Scintillating dust, they disappeared.

So the pale family closed all their windows, their work done. They set the house key under a stone outside. They did the same next door for Thom; for Thom had gone.

On a still night, late in summer, they left. Three figures: boy, mother, father. All the men and women of the village knew they'd gone. They'd watched them pass from their half-open windows, while the children played on the streets scooping up the silvery-gold dust, polishing their faces.

That September two new families moved to the sandstone village, into those clean, empty houses. Filled with light, side by side. The disappearance of the old man Thom remained unexplained. Something important had happened in the sandstone village, said the voices of the men and the women and the children. Silvery-gold dust could be found, throughout the village, in small soft drifts, for years.

MERMAID'S PURSE

Patricia Roberts

Tears stinging behind her eyes, Milly sat on the edge of the harbour wall. The gritty edge scratched against her sunburned legs, matching the way her whole body seemed to burn with the injustice of the morning so far.

"You know you're the eldest, you should keep an eye on your little brother ... "

"You know Jake's too little to find his own way back from the rock pools. You should stay with him."

"Why is your head always stuck inside a book ... ?"

There had been five minutes of panic, with mum shading her eyes and desperately scanning the beach. Neighbouring families, curious behind their windbreaks, had seemed to rather welcome the diversion of the search for a curly-haired five-year-old in a grey t-shirt. In the end it was Milly who had discovered Jake, slightly hidden behind a rock, earnestly piling shells on top of a lopsided heap of sand and muttering urgently to himself. Totally unaware of the drama he had caused, he presented Milly with a handful of shells and treasures and allowed himself to be led back up the beach.

Now he was cuddled in mum's arms and sucking on an ice lolly. No doubt in a minute he would be asleep and mum would be telling the nearby family, in a voice shaky with relief and pride, what a wonderful imagination he had.

Milly banged her sandals against the harbour wall and gradually became more aware of the sounds around her. Two boys were dangling crab lines into the water and shrieking in delight at their success. In a yellow plastic bucket, trapped crabs scrambled over each other, trying to hook a claw over the yellow plastic to freedom. The older boy showed off a little as he demonstrated just how to hold a crab without being nipped. Their father bent over the boys, pointing out things on the shells and Milly heard him telling his sons how to tell a male crab from a female. She knew what was coming next.

"OK, lads, it's not fair to keep them in the bucket for too long: they'll get too warm. Put them back in the sea now."

The bucket was tipped gently and the crabs hovered for a moment on the surface of the water before gliding down to hide amongst the waving fronds of seaweed. Milly wondered idly if crabs could learn a lesson, or whether these same ones would find themselves swinging out of the water tomorrow, tricked again by a lump of bacon on the end of a string.

As the boys and their dad wandered off towards the beach and their lunch, Milly was left alone and, just for a moment, the sky seemed to darken as the sun went behind a cloud. She tucked her hands up the sleeves of her fleece and rubbed her arms as she sat, swinging her legs on the harbour wall. She peered into the water hoping that the newly released crabs had found the perfect hiding place. The seaweed waved slowly with the water in green and brown strands and, as she stared, its movement made her feel calmer, quieter, almost mesmerising her.

The familiar sounds of the seaside grew fainter. Children's shouts, seagulls' screeches, beach games – all became just a murmur. The lapping, hypnotic sound of the sea filled Milly's head completely now as she stared down at the moving mass beneath the surface of the sea. She was unable to tear her eyes away.

Then she heard the song.

Mermaid's Purse

Notes rippled all around Milly as she continued to look into the green sea. The music was different from any she had ever heard before. It wasn't a tune, more a silvery rippling sound that filled her head and entranced her, making her hope it never would end. As the music enfolded her, suddenly everything seemed alright again. Mum's harsh words no longer seemed to matter; she no longer blamed herself for Jake getting lost. In fact, as a strange feeling of happiness flooded through her, Milly knew with a calm certainty that only the music and the lapping water mattered to her now.

The sea began to swirl and a slender, perfectly white arm rose from the sea. Water streamed from it and it shimmered with an eerie light. A long pale finger beckoned. Milly, head filled with music, rose. Standing there surrounded by music and sea, she had no idea how she had got to her feet. Her body was compelled by a powerful force, and now she wanted to follow where the arm was leading.

As she stood on the harbour edge, a slight figure, enticed and entranced, the clouds parted and the sun shone brightly on the sea. The water sparkled and the white arm glimmered. Then, in the corner of her eye, Milly saw a shadow, a small, curly-haired shadow with an outstretched arm. In her dreamlike state she was not sure for a moment why Jake should be there. As she turned to face the shadow, the music seemed to grow discordant for a moment, but then the sweetness returned. Jake stomped towards her on his short plump legs. His face was still sticky from the ice lolly as, smiling, he reached out a grubby hand to his sister.

Milly hesitated.

Eyes gritty with sand or tears, she held the sticky hand as they made their way back to their mother on the beach. She had a strange sadness, a feeling that she had lost something that she would never be able to get back again. And yet, she had a sense that she had gained something, something somehow too complicated to put into words or properly understand.

Scattered on the blanket on their spot on the beach were Jake's shells and treasures. Amongst the limpet shells, coloured stones and scraps of seaweed lay a thick, leathery pouch. It was a dogfish egg case. When it was held up to the sun the 'pearl' of the dogfish egg could be seen, nestled in its case.

"Hey, Jake", whispered Milly, "They call these mermaids' purses."

"Well, we must give it back to the mermaid," he replied, wide eyed.

Hand in hand they raced to the water's edge. Milly pulled her arm right back and threw the purse into the sea in a wide, arching throw. Turning to lead Jake back up the beach she took one last look over her shoulder. As discordant sounds filled her head she saw a cold, white, hand disappear under the waves.

FAKE BLOOD AND BULLIES

Rosamund Roberts

Monday 3:30 p.m.
I was waiting for my Mum when Danny Myers walked past. I tried to look busy, rummaging in my rucksack. I should have been looking for my front door key but I can't have a key. Not until I'm 12. So I have to wait on the stupid wall for Mum to get home from work.

"It was your lunch money I took, wan' it?" said Danny. His mates, the pillars, grunted. The pillars grunt a lot and carry Danny's bag. They are called Wacco and Baz. Actually, their real names are Wayne and Barry but only the teachers call them that.

My mum doesn't like Danny Myers because he spits and wears his trousers so low you can see his pants. But he is far worse than that. He slams toilet doors on kids and steals dinner money. He'd stolen mine that very Monday. I gave it to him, every penny. He won't do it again. Not after what happened that week.

Danny flicked my rucksack. I climbed off the wall and walked down the side path but the gate was locked. The pillars blocked the way back.

"Can't get in?" said Danny. And then my mum came home from work, which was both a relief and embarrassing.

"Hello boys," she said as if they were about to come for tea. They disappeared.

"I do wish those boys would pull their trousers up," said mum and she opened the front door.

Tuesday 3:30 p.m.
They were nasty on Tuesday.

"Got any money?" said Danny. I shook my head.

"Nowt to say?" he said.

"Got any decent mates?" I said. It just came out of my mouth. The pillars were not happy.

"I'll have him, Danny," said Baz.

But Danny had turned quiet and his face was pinched. "Don't you think you're the clever un," he said. He came up close. He smelt of chips. "Real clever with the jokes." He pushed me. Not just a gentle push but a real jab that hit my ribs. I fell against the wall. "We'll be back tomorrow and you better have cash. No-one tries to be clever with me."

They left. I tried to make a joke to myself about the pillars but I was rattled. Properly rattled. It was stupid to rattle Danny Myers.

Wednesday
I had football after school so I was late home. Saved.

Thursday 3:30 p.m.
They came for their cash. But my mum came home at the same time. She was with her troop to practise their play, her friend Margery leading the way with a bag of daggers. They were two days from performing their Greek tragedy at the village hall. Eight of them paraded down the side path and I tagged on the end. I turned round and Danny was staring straight at me. 'Tomorrow' he mouthed and I knew he meant it.

I was quite scared and so for the first time ever I actually helped them practise their stupid play. This stunned my mother into gushing happiness. I normally completely ignore her fellow actors as among them is Dave. Dave is my mum's boyfriend. He has bad feet and keeps slapping me on the back and calling me 'mate'. The first time he stayed over

Mermaid's Purse

I bumped into him coming out of the bathroom. He was wearing superhero boxer shorts and an old t-shirt of my Dad's that said 'Relax, Don't do it'.

"I think my Dad might need that," I said to him and I've said very little to him ever since.

Funny thing is, that day, Dave seemed to tell I was rattled.

"You alright, Ben?" he asked. I nodded. I was sitting on the sofa, flicking through the script. Dave was wearing a sheet wrapped like a toga and his bad feet were in sandals which made them really bad.

"Those lads bothering you?" he said.

I shrugged.

"One of them mouthed 'tomorrow'. What did he mean?"

I whirled round and stared at Dave. He always seemed so gawky and odd. It amazed me that he knew something was up.

"Dave," called my mother. "It's time for you to die!"

Dave raised his eyes to the ceiling.

"After I've died, we'll chat."

They practised the death scene in the back garden. There were daggers and fake blood and, for the first two attempts, it was hard not to laugh. The blood gushed too much and Dave staggered into one of mum's plant pots and snapped the daffodil heads. By the third and fourth go they had the timing sorted. On the fifth, it was fairly scary and the dagger and the blood and Dave's death gave me a faint shiver. My mother of course, shed tears.

Dave said they could stop. (He is not only chief Greek but Director.) Mum dashed into the house and returned with a cloth to wipe the blood from her veggie patch. Strange, really. Dad wasn't even allowed to wash his boots in the back garden and yet she lets Dave spray blood on the courgettes.

Dave pulled me to one side.

"What time tomorrow?"

"What do you mean?"

"What time are those lads coming tomorrow?"

"About 3:30," I said.

And then Dave winked at me and told everyone to be at Mum's house, the next day 3:00 sharp. No costumes so they could be cleaned and ready for opening night.

Dave stayed that night. For the first time it didn't feel strange. And for the first time we talked and I told him quite a lot of stuff.

Friday 3:30 p.m.
They came and I was ready on the wall. Danny was in a bad mood. He was strutting and spitting, hands deep in pockets, the pillars several paces behind. It felt like the air was sucked dry of anything good. I looked down the side path and gave Dave the thumbs up. He shut the gate.

"You better have it," said Danny. The pillars took a step forward.

"You need to follow me," I said.

Danny Myers is not used to being told to do things.

"I," he said, poking me, "need to follow – you? Yeah, right." He grabbed my arm. Dave's plan was failing. I told him it wouldn't work.

But, at that very moment, a blacked-out car crawled up beside us and stopped. This had not been part of the plan. The exhaust spluttered and rap music churned from inside. The door opened and a huge guy covered in tattoos heaved himself out. He was wearing leather. The passenger door opened and out stepped a guy with gold teeth and knuckle-

Mermaid's Purse

dusters. Something was familiar about him. The two men towered over Baz and Wacco.

"Are you Danny Myers?" the tattooed one asked.

We both stared at him, stunned. He knew Danny's name. Danny grabbed the wall.

"Yes," he said.

"Been hearing about the dinner money stuff, Danny," said the one with the gold teeth. "Wondering if we need to have a word?"

Danny glanced at me.

"Wasn't 'im told us."

The man grimaced and the gold gleamed. And then I knew who it was. Margery Davenport's son, the dentist. He had dropped off the tickets for the play.

"My niece told me. And if I get told anyfing like that again, we'll be waiting. Got it?" On the 'anyfing' bit, his roughness had started to slip but Danny didn't seem to notice. He nodded and shuffled down the side path, the pillars following.

Now the fun really started. We opened the gate and at that moment Dave, dressed in biker jeans and ripped shirt began his line to start the Greek tragedy fight. Not a toga or sandal in sight. Just two men, vicious and angry and ready to kill. Margery Davenport screamed. A knife appeared. The baddy lunged. Dave fell back and grabbed his stomach. The blood oozed through his t-shirt. Danny screamed. Actually screamed. Wacco fell against Mum's trellis and got tangled in the wisteria. Baz ran away. Well, he tried to but Margery Davenport had locked the gate and he couldn't get out.

"Oh my God!" yelled Danny. He turned and fled, tripping over Wacco as he went. The three of them were now pinned against the gate, a string of wisteria sticking out of Wacco's hair. Baz was panting like a dog.

And then one by one the actors stood up and went into the house. Dave was the last, peeling himself up from the floor. He went inside and closed the door. It really was their best performance.

Margery Davenport unlocked the gate. She smiled at Danny and handed him a leaflet advertising the play. Danny retched slightly and then the three boys fled, like rabbits.

Danny Myers won't bother me again. I'm pretty sure of that. And Dave is alright really. He's even convincing Mum to give me a key. He just needs some new boxer shorts and his feet sorted and then we may possibly have a future sharing my mum.

THE EXTRAORDINARY INVENTIONS OF VICTOR VANASH

Lisa Jane Rowlands

This is a story
Of triumph and glory
Of good ousting wicked intentions
And how boys from my school
Who were crooked and cruel
Fell victim to Victor's inventions

It was the start of Year Seven
I had just turned eleven
When I chanced upon Victor Vanash
He was awkward and thin
With a long, pointed chin
And the roots of a thick, black moustache

I was chubby and spotty
My hair was all knotty
And I tripped on my tongue when I spoke
I was painfully shy
And so Victor and I
Became butts of the other boys' jokes

They would call us both names
They'd exclude us from games
They would poke us and pinch us in class
They'd hide our possessions
And gesture in lessons
To make sure we knew we were 'Trash'

Wordlife

The chief guilty party
Was Mike Moriarty
He'd pelt us with bottles and stones
Then he'd force us to shower
In raw eggs and flour
Whilst other boys filmed on their phones

We were humbled and saddened
Frustrated and maddened
But thoughts of revenge would be barmy
I mean, what could we do
With our legion of two
Against Mike and his hooligan army?

If we tried to fight back
With our feeble attack
It would just make them bully us more
So we chose to confine
To the backs of our minds
Any notions of settling the score ...

Then one afternoon
As we sat in his room
Watching cricket on ESPN
Victor casually mentioned
His latest inventions
Then opened the doors to his den

It was a playground of dreams
There were robots in teams
Dodging balls that you can't see or hear
There were self-writing inks

The Extraordinary Inventions

And absorbable drinks
And a cream that makes things disappear!

There were infinite ices
And hi-tech devices
That transform your thoughts into words
And skyscraper shelves
Where the books read themselves
Aboard bikes that fly faster than birds!

There were things of all kinds
Some that mess with your mind
And some that cast shadows of fear
That could tender a taste
Of the foods that we've faced
To the boys that had plagued us all year

So armed with this vision
We embarked on our mission
And marched with intent into school
Our bag of tricks brimming
With lesson one: swimming
The first battlefield was the pool

We smiled as the rest
Of our classmates undressed
Then with vanishing cream on our hands
We swiftly applied
To their trousers and ties
Their blazers, their shirts and their pants!

Wordlife

Some trembled in fear
As their clothes disappeared
Some grumbled, some grimaced, some howled
And Mike and his chums
Sat and cried for their mums
Wearing nothing but trunks and a towel!

We were stunned and surprised
That these self-styled 'tough guys'
Could at once become weak as can be
And the cream on the cake
Is that each single take
Had been captured on CCTV!

… We are now in Year Nine
We've been free for some time
And we each have our own new intentions
Mine: to pen stories
Of Triumph and Glory
And Victor's: to make more inventions!

ARTHUR AND THE MOUNTAIN

Nicola Russell-Johnson

(So you want a story do you? You came here wanting a story? Are you sure you don't want to know the number 45 bus timetable instead? No? Alright then, I will tell you a story. I will tell you a story that my grandfather once told me; perhaps it is the time to pass it on.)

In a place really far away, there is a village at the bottom of a mountain. And at the top of the mountain is a dark castle.

(Isn't that always the way?)

Now in this small village is a boy called Arthur. And he's not behaving himself.

(That's always the way too.)

Now Arthur, he's pretty disgusting because he's been playing in the muck, so when he gets home and his mother sees him, he's going to be in big trouble. But you know what happens?

NOTHING

Nothing happens.

His mother opens her mouth, and no words come out. She tries to yell at him. But no matter how much she tries to get those words out, she cannot utter a thing. Arthur's mother is starting to go a little pink. She's trying that hard.

Next Arthur's dad comes out. He wants to see why everything has gone quiet. You see he'd been expecting Arthur's mother to yell.

He tries to say: "Is everything alright?" and "Arthur, What's going on?"

Wordlife

But NOTHING at all comes out of his mouth. He can't speak either. So Arthur, he gets worried. He runs out of the house and finds that everyone is standing in the street speechless. Because no one can say a word. Not even the word 'dangly.'

(And that's a really good word.)

Now Arthur's grandpa lives close by. So Arthur runs like mad to his grandpa's house, because although Arthur's grandpa is a bit fuzzy round the edges, he's actually quite smart. And Arthur reckons he might have an idea what's going on.

Arthur runs.

All the streets are silent. It's a bit like someone with a giant TV remote has put the mute button on the village.

Hold this page to your ear. Go on.
Can you hear anything?
No?
See, I told you it was silent.

When Arthur gets to grandpa's house, his grandpa opens the door and he says: "Come in Arthur."

And well, even if Arthur could talk, he'd be speechless, because fuzzy old grandpa is the only person who can speak. Grandpa looks at Arthur. He's expecting to have 'HELLO GRANDPA' bellowed at him. But grandpa doesn't hear a thing. He takes his hearing aid out and checks he's got it switched on. He gives it a bit of a rattle too because shaking things vigorously sometimes gets them working again.

Then grandpa looks outside, then he looks at Arthur and then he says, "I've been preparing for this."

He leads Arthur into his kitchen. Grandpa's kitchen is very small with a giant white fridge in it. He opens up the big white door. And Arthur stares at what's inside. Because

Arthur and the Mountain

grandpa's fridge is stuffed full, and it's not stuffed full of kippers or haddock. It's full of words. Some really long words like DISCOMBOOMERATE and FLOCCINAUCINIHILIPILIFICATION are folded up and stored in the freezer compartment, while all the really small words like IT and OR are balled up like peas.

Grandpa has a particularly well-spoken fridge.

"I keep a store," says Arthur's grandpa. "That way I'm never lost for words."

And it's true, Arthur's grandpa pretty much had an answer to everything.

"You see when I was young, I came home one day, just like you, and nobody could talk! So I went to visit my grandpa, Grandpa Goldstein, just like you too! (Although I did it with much better dress sense.) And you know what happened when I went to Grandpa Goldstein's house and couldn't talk?"

Arthur reaches into the fridge and chooses the word, "What?"

"Nothing! Grandpa Goldstein didn't notice I couldn't talk! Grandpa Goldstein was deaf as a post! Grandpa Goldstein hadn't heard a thing since a trip to France in 1917. But I did spot something strange in his kitchen. There, hidden behind a jar of pickled cabbage, keeping cool, was the word MOUNTAIN! And the moment I read it, I accidentally shouted it out. MOUNTAIN! Just like that!"

And then, because it had been really rather nice to shout MOUNTAIN, Arthur's grandpa roots about in the fridge for another MOUNTAIN to shout. Although by mistake he grabs the word RHINOCEROS and shouts that instead, which is almost as good a word to shout out as MOUNTAIN, at a push.

Wordlife

"But you see," says Arthur's grandpa after he'd finished shouting RHINOCEROS, "because I shouted it out, it escaped and then I was back to not being able to speak again. There were no more words in Grandpa Goldstein's kitchen! There were a couple of herrings but there weren't any more words at all!"

Arthur digs about for some more words, "So what did you do?"

"Well," says Arthur's grandpa, "I decided that Grandpa Goldstein must have put that word MOUNTAIN safe in his kitchen for a reason. So you know what I did? I climbed the MOUNTAIN! And there, at the top, at the very top, I found something very interesting indeed!"

Arthur looks puzzled and he reads a word which is in one of the round holes meant for eggs in the fridge, and he uses it. He says "WHAT?"

Grandpa says, "You must find out. You've got to climb the mountain Arthur. You've got to climb the mountain because my old legs just won't take me up there anymore."

So Arthur runs home and gets a really comfy pair of shoes and a bag. He hurries back to grandpa's to stock up on some words for a few conversations. He finds that grandpa has prepared two lunch boxes and is waiting by the fridge so they can talk.

"Here," he says, with a fresh bunch of words from the crisper. "Here are two lunch boxes. This one contains a very important sentence. You must only open this when the time is right."

"What about the other one?" asks Arthur.

"The other one contains a beetroot and marmalade sandwich. You must only open this if you feel like a light snack on the way up."

Arthur and the Mountain

So Arthur pulls the bag onto his shoulders and begins to climb up the mountain, and after a while he feels hungry. But when he pulls out his lunch boxes he really doesn't know which box is which. It's when he's trying to see through the opaque plastic lunch boxes that Arthur hears, "Are there any flies in there?"

Arthur looks up, all he sees is a particularly warty toad.

"What's the matter, cat got your tongue?"

"Pardon me?" says Arthur. "Did you ask if I had any flies in here?"

The toad says, "Yes, shocking isn't it, we really do eat them. Quite, quite revolting, but one can't go against one's nature I suppose."

Arthur roots about for the words HOLY SHAMOLY in his bag, but turns out his Grandpa hadn't collected those ones, so instead he says quite calmly, "I've never met a talking toad before."

"Don't get out much do you?"

Arthur doesn't think this is worth wasting any of his words on, so he just glares at the toad instead.

"Everyone round here can talk. The castle has started to leak words. There are so many even the goldfish in the moat come to the surface in the evening to discuss the weather."

In fact the toad goes on to tell Arthur that when he was just a tadpole he grew up in a whole pond of words. He says that his entire family can talk and that his sister, a terribly ambitious natterjack, is currently studying accounting in Ramsbottom.

Then the toad agrees to take Arthur to where the words leak out and after a long, long climb, Arthur and the toad reach the castle. The castle is so busy looming that its drawbridge is pulled up and the dark moat that surrounds it looks very unpleasant. In fact when the toad shows Arthur his word pond home, Arthur discovers that it is made out of words like SMELLY and STAGNANT and SYRUPY, which are not particularly nice words.

(Well, syrupy is not so bad as long as it's being used to describe syrup.)

Arthur has to cross the moat, but he can't think of a way that doesn't involve wading through it. And then he has an idea. He roots through the word pond until he finds what he's looking for. He fishes out the words FLOAT and BUOYANCY AID and attaches them to his feet by the words STRING and TWINE. This way Arthur floats to the castle door.

Inside the castle is dank and dark. Hiding in the shadows are frightening words like GHOUL and LURK. When Arthur sees the word SPOOK, it's so scary he wants to turn and run.

At the end of the gloomy corridor is a staircase. Arthur climbs and climbs. He climbs so high that the word ALTITUDE SICKNESS sticks to his head. And just when Arthur is feeling a little dizzy he reaches a big heavy door.

Arthur pushes hard against the door and it opens with a deafening Eeeeeeeeeeeeeeeeeeekkkkkkkkkkkkkkkkkkkk!

Inside is an old, old man. He lifts his head and says, "Who are you?"

Arthur says, "I'm Arthur."

"Ahhh, I suppose you want me to make more words?"

"Yes," says Arthur.

"Well I'm not going to. I'm not making any more words and that's that."

"Why?" asks Arthur.

"I've made enough words for the world to speak for years."

"But no one can speak!" says Arthur.

Arthur and the Mountain

"I've made so many words that all the unused ones had to hibernate."

Arthur has just one sentence in his bag left and this is it, "Where are they hibernating?"

And the old man shouts so loud he nearly falls over, "IN BOOKS! You just need to read them. I'm not going to make any new words until people start waking up the old ones!"

Arthur searches for stray words, but all he finds are lunch boxes. Then Arthur remembers the words in the lunchbox. He opens one, it's a marmalade and beetroot sandwich.

He opens the other, it's a big fat natterjack the size of a cream cheese bagel, who has eaten grandpa's words.

People are silent because nobody reads any more.

And just then the toad belches and he burps out the words:

"WHAT DO YOU THINK YOU ARE DOING RIGHT NOW?"

HESTER'S HANDS

Beverley Sims

On a tiny island far away from here, a girl called Hester lived with her father. He had once been a great juggler with a famous circus, and he could still spin plates on stripy poles whilst riding a unicycle. Their home, Whirly House, was unlike any of the others because it sat on a little rock of its own, attached to the island by a bridge made of rope. It was red and white and swirly, like a giant raspberry ripple ice-cream.

But what was particularly special about Hester and her father was how they spoke to each other. Using sign language. Their faces, fingers and hands took the place of spoken words, because Hester was deaf. She could not hear the song of the seagulls or the roar of the ocean, but she understood the words of the other islanders by watching how they moved their lips. Hester made normal words dance in such a beautiful way, that soon everybody on the island could use sign language.

Hester would often sit for hours in a little cave looking out at the sea and remembering the circus days, the cherry-nosed clowns, the flame-throwers and the strongmen. And her mother. Most of all she remembered her mother, dressed in a thousand tiny stars, gliding through the air on her glittering trapeze. With each swing of the bar, she would wave down to her daughter from the spangled ceiling of the tent, and made Hester feel as though every performance was especially for her.

That was before the night of the terrible fire. It had raged through the circus tent like a wild beast, devouring everything that got in its way. The performers and the

Hester's Hands

spectators had scattered like marbles in every direction, but her mother was trapped on the trapeze. She hadn't got out alive.

Their loss was so dreadful that Hester and her father moved far away, to a land where skies were blue and air was fresh. But she never forgot. Here in the secret cave she kept hidden her most treasured possession. A small velvet bag of glittering stars and sequins that her mother had planned to sew onto her next costume, and which Hester loved with all her heart.

Each week a huge market on the island attracted visitors from across the turquoise ribbon of sea, and some stayed for a holiday. One afternoon as her father was juggling with tiny wooden lighthouses, Hester talked with some of the islanders using her special language. Two boys were watching. They pointed and sneered and made fun of her. Then one of them stole her bag of juggling balls and threw them to the other. Hester was very angry and stomped over.

"Why did you do that?" she signed. But the boys didn't understand her, and only sniggered.

"Are you stupid, or something?" one of them smirked, not caring that she had understood every word.

Soon the islanders began to complain of mysterious troubles on their usually peaceful haven by the sea. Delicate shell wind-chimes were snapped off doorframes and crushed, gardens were trampled, and pebbles were hurled through greenhouse windows. Each and every day they sighed as they picked up more broken pieces of their beloved island, hoping that the troublemakers would stop.

One Market Day Hester and her father left early because of the sudden change in the weather, and as they approached Whirly House, they saw a truly terrible sight. Their home was no longer a summery swirl of red and white, but a broken tower of blue and black graffiti, with all the windows smashed. They couldn't even reach it on its little rock as the old rope bridge had been cut down and now lay unravelled on the sand below in a giant salty coil.

"What do we do?" asked Hester, tears pricking her eyes. Her father told her not to worry, but to wait in her cave until he got back with the island police.

Hester ran quickly but the pebbles beneath her feet were slippery as fish. The clouds tumbled overhead like great dark fists ready to fight, and fat fingers of rain fell into her eyes. Inside the cave she had another shock. Empty cartons surrounded a smouldering campfire and smeared across the walls in the same blue and black paint, was more graffiti. Her heart pounded with panic as she remembered her bag of sequins. "Please, please let it be there" she thought as she lifted up the rock where it was usually kept. But it had gone.

First Hester was furious, and then upset and then she began to feel afraid. She didn't want to stay here alone, and decided to head towards the town. As she hurried along the cliff she noticed something moving in the blustery sea. Shielding her eyes from the rain, she saw two figures clinging to a tiny rock, their hands waving wildly. In no time at all they would be swallowed up completely by the tide.

Hester remembered the fire at the circus, and knew how quickly terror could grip the heart and paralyse the legs. She had to do something!

She ran down to the rope in the sand below and tried to lift it, but the rain had made it too heavy. Suddenly she noticed something in the distance. A long line of lanterns carried by the islanders, and led by her father. Hester shouted, using the voice she herself had never heard. But the roar of the wind was too loud. So using the biggest signals

Hester's Hands

she could, she waved and jumped until she got their attention.

Holding up their lamps they recognised Hester's distress, and understood from her signs what was happening out at sea. Her father hurried down the cliff and shouted back to the locals, but the wild wind whipped away his words. So, like his daughter, he used exaggerated signs and gestures to explain what the islanders should do.

Soon they had formed a long line stretching far back, with the heavy rope looped between them. At one end was a burly fisherman with hands like barnacled anchors, and at the other end was Hester's father. His years as a juggler and an acrobat had made him strong and wiry, and he waded into the water up to his chest, where the terrified boys were shivering on the rock. He pulled them into his arms, and told them to hang on. Then with the rope wound tightly around him, the islanders began to pull them through the rage of the water and back towards to the shore. Anyone stood on the cliff that dark and stormy night would have seen a long line of people rising like a giant sea-snake from the waves.

Hester and her father slept at the fisherman's cottage that night, and when they arose the following morning the sun was already sizzling high in the sky. Although Hester was relieved that the boys were safe, her heart was heavy as a stone when she remembered Whirly House with all its black graffiti.

On their way home Hester noticed something strange. Each islander they passed smiled and said hello, but not one of them signed to her. In fact their hands were definitely not on show at all. Hidden behind their backs or in their pockets, they remained oddly out of view.

And then Hester saw why. Whirly House had been completely transformed. The angry black marks had disappeared; the windows had been repaired and there was even a brand new rope bridge. Surf white and decorated with tiny starfishes of colour, from coral pink to seahorse green, the house looked like a giant ice-cream cone covered in hundreds and thousands. Perched on ladders and steps, the islanders were still busy painting. But instead of using brushes, they were making handprints. And when they turned and waved Hester could see their brightly painted palms.

Standing at the bottom of Whirly House, their hands coloured lilac and blue, were the two boys. They seemed smaller and younger than they had before. The older one came to Hester and smiled nervously. He wiped his hands, and pulled the velvet bag from his pocket. It was empty. Then he made a sign. The sign for 'Sorry'.

The biggest surprise was still to come when Hester finally returned to the cave. Gone was the smoky fire and the litter. Gone was the dark graffiti. Instead, wedged into the walls and the roof, were the precious sequins, dancing and glittering like a billion stars. Hester twirled around and around looking up at the sparkling constellation in astonishment.

It reminded her of heaven. Or of a long-ago spangled circus tent, where a beautiful woman had once smiled down from a shimmering trapeze.

FOREVERMORE

Andrew Smith

Outside...when you grow up in the Dome, you don't ever want to think about outside.

Outside the sky is always red. The land is grey and brown and cracked. There are no plants or water, nothing alive. And the air is like fire.

The Dome protects us from outside. In the Dome we are safe.

My family were all gone. I lived alone in an apartment on the eighty-third floor of Worker Building One. In my sister's old room I went to the closet and pulled out bags and bags of her abandoned clothes and shoes, revealing the floorboards below. One of them was loose and I pulled it away, then reached my hand into the darkness below and pulled out the book.

A month ago I had found this hiding place and the small red book hidden inside it. I had read it so many times that it was as familiar as an old nursery rhyme. After each reading I had hidden it away again. It had to be hidden. It was dangerous. It was a secret book, not something you'd find in any library or shop.

I slipped the book into my jacket and took a final look around the apartment, then left without even bothering to lock the door. I walked to the nearest cage and hit the button for the ground floor. On the wall of the shuddering cage was a painting of the Leader. There are always paintings of him in the Dome, everywhere you look, pictures of a small man with too much skin, like a slowly deflating balloon.

When the cage stopped I walked out into the quiet streets. I could feel the book pressing against me and it was comforting to know it was there, even though taking it out was the riskiest thing I had ever done.

The sky was blue and perfect. It is always perfect in the Dome, because it is not *really* the sky; it is a computer image. If you stare up for long enough you will see that birds flock the same way each and every time. The clouds come and go in cycles that never change. I designed many of those clouds myself and stopped now to try to remember what they were based on. I found a rabbit and a whale before I started walking again.

Further down the street I watched a group of Controllers (big men in big, black uniforms carrying big, black batons who ran the Dome for the Leader) stop a car and make the man and woman inside get out and answer questions. They looked so scared I could almost *feel* it. The Controllers found something bad in the car and the woman started crying. The man, too. The controllers took them away in the back of a truck and I knew they were going to the same place my sister had, the same place my parents had been taken many years ago.

They said my parents were traitors.

That was why they were taken behind the Black Wall. The Black Wall is prison. It is a huge wall that cuts off an entire section of the Dome. Once you go there you never come back. There are no displays behind the Black Wall, so you have to see the real sky. You live in camps with only basic food and people steal and fight. There are no rules, no law, no safety.

Years later, they called my sister a traitor, also, and she was taken behind the Black Wall too.

But not me. The Leader and the Controllers needed me. You see, they don't like people to be too clever, so school is

Forevermore

for training you to be loyal to the Leader, nothing more, so he can continue to be...well, the leader.

But for some people, just a few, it's different. Like me. I understood computers and images, colours and shapes, light and shade, like most people understood how to breathe. I was trained to program the massive computer displays that cover the inside of the Dome. That's my job. Why? Because it keeps people happy so they can forget the truth of the real world outside the Dome. And happy people, forgetful people, do not do things like my family did. Happy and forgetful people do not stand up against our Leader who rules everything in our lives. Happy and forgetful people do not say, "This is wrong!"

Happy and forgetful people do not get sent behind the Black Wall.

But I have read the book many times now. It is called *Forevermore*, and every single page says "THIS IS WRONG!"

The book made me understand why my parents decided to say it too, and why my sister (who must have found the book hidden in my parents' things) did the same. And I think they were right to do it! But their voices were small ...

Ten minutes later I reached Control Tower Two, where I worked. Inside, two Controllers scanned my eyes for security, then I took the cage up to the Display Lab on level 112. Inside were cold metal walls, bright lights and computers. On the screens were designs for birds, clouds, sunrises and sets. In this room I controlled the way the sky looked.

I sat at my desk and carefully took the book out of my jacket, like it was burning hot. Some birds flew across the sky outside my window and I tried to imagine what *real* birds must have looked like, before they became extinct. I tried to imagine zooming in on them through a telescope, but in my imagination the closer I got to them the more they became a rough collection of black blocks. Because they were not birds, they were just a computer image. It was a beautiful lie I told everyone in the Dome. And most people were happy to pretend they believed me.

I turned on my computer and started my plan.

I stood on the roof of Control Tower Two. There were buildings as far as the eye could see, grey, grey, grey against the blue sky. The Black Wall was far off and I turned my back on it.

At seven PM the siren sounded. The workday had finished. I looked down at the streets below and saw thousands of people leaving work buildings.

Less than a minute to go.

I breathed deeply to calm myself and stared up at the fake sky for the last time. They would take me behind the Black Wall after this.

Five, four, three, two, one …

It was time.

The sky suddenly turned black, there was a flash of white, and then *Forevermore* filled the Dome, each page scanned and displayed, the words so large they looked like clouds made of black, twisted rope.

I could hear the people on the streets gasp and shout. I read the sky: *"This is wrong. We must all say it, and say it together, or things will never change, and we shall be scared forevermore."*

The Black Wall loomed over me as I stood in front of it with a Controller holding me so I could not run away. A door, like a mouth in the wall's terrible face, lifted with a sound like distant thunder and the Controller pushed me through the opening. The door slammed shut behind me.

Forevermore

I was behind the Black Wall. My eyes blinked and my mouth fell open because it was not as I had expected. Confusion made me tremble. There was no more Dome above me. I was not in a prison camp. I was outside, in the *real world*! But it was not red and black, cracked and broken. No, it was a sea of colour. And it was not poisoned. I took in lungfuls of sweet, fresh air.

Understanding slowly came as I felt a strange sensation and realised it was a breeze. Everything in the Dome was fake, a lie. In the Dome, the Leader had power because we all thought we *had* to stay in the Dome. But that was a lie, too, so he could keep his power and continue to be ... well, the Leader.

I looked all around me, excited and scared at the same time.

I started to walk, sometimes quickly to find other people, sometimes slowly to touch the grass and trees. In the sky, the *real* sky, there were birds, and I knew that if I got close enough to them they would not become collections of tiny dots like a computer image, but they would be beautiful and clear. And the clouds! Each one was different! And if I stopped and watched them, they would change and I would never see the same exact shape twice.

Far off I saw a plume of smoke. I headed off in that direction.

THE EVACUEE

Naomi Walker

War was over, yet still I remained
Waiting to be collected.
"Not long now, love,"
They said to me
Hoping I was reassured.

The countryside was part of me now,
No longer alien.
London, a distant memory.
Would they still know me?
I wondered.

The last time I saw them
Was on my birthday.
Visitors, they were.
Dad on leave,
Mum on holiday.

Laughs, smiles,
We shared them all.
Then, when they left,
I cried.
All alone.

"See you soon"
They said. "Won't be long."
It was.
Two hundred and sixty-nine days.
Eleven minutes.

The Evacuee

I hated it when I first came.
Didn't like the dirt
And fresh air.
Collect eggs now, I do,
And muck out the animals.

"Proper country girl"
They now call me,
Instead of the awful names they did at first,
Like "town rat" and
Worse.

Friends I've made,
Dorrie, Maud and Ellie.
Playing hopscotch and
Skipping.
Oranges and Lemons.

School's all right now too.
Know all my Kings and Queens
And can count backwards
From one hundred
In twos.

I've grown two inches.
Mrs Betts had to take my hem down.
Put a ribbon round the edge
To stop it fraying.
Looks awful pretty.

"They won't recognise you,"
She says.
I bite back tears.

Wordlife

Pretend I'm coughing.
"Hope you're not ill."

I hear a plane.
Maybe Father is coming to fetch me.
It disappears,
Sound fading like the breeze.
All still.

Not long now,
We'll all be together again soon.
Maybe here,
Maybe there.
A family.

LION

Stephen Wrigley

Deep in my imagination,
farthest point of inner eye,
there is a shadow. A lion
gazes at me, paces by.

He is tawny, long legged, lazy;
dozes, twitches, flicks his ear.
But if I fail to concentrate,
shadows shift. He disappears

and I feel lost. He is my friend,
fiercely fights my corner, wins,
brushes obstacles aside,
lets me catch him up. We grin.

Close to sleep I sense him by me,
turn my face into his fur.
The mountains of his muscles tremble,
rumble, rise and fall. He purrs.

But I grow up. The images –
tail lash then the sudden charge,
diminish as the plains of
my forgetfulness stretch large.

Left unimagined, left unloved,
a lion stiffens in his limbs.
The thorn that pricks his paw festers,
fierceness in his eye dims.

Wordlife

Savannas beckon. Dust storms swirl.
Rivers swell from flash flood streams.
He pads away, the briefest turn
mere outline in a distant dream.

There is a lion by the house,
stone guard, crouching on all fours.
His gaze is steady, measured, bold.
Odd, he has a broken paw.

Standing by his side I hear
the echo of a big cat purr.
A shadow tracks the inner eye
and prowls into my heart.